A S H L E Y
F A R L E Y

Beyond
the
Garden

MAGNOLIA SERIES

ALSO BY ASHLEY FARLEY

Sweet Tea Tuesdays

Saving Ben

Sweeney Sisters Series

Saturdays at Sweeney's

Tangle of Strings

Boots and Bedlam

Lowcountry Stranger

Her Sister's Shoes

Magnolia Series

Magnolia Nights

Adventures of Scottie

Breaking the Story

Merry Mary

Cover design: damonza.com

Editor: Patricia Peters at A Word Affair LLC

Leisure Time Books, a division of AHF Publishing All rights reserved. No part
of this book may be used or reproduced in any manner without written
permission from the author.

ISBN: 978-0-9982741-6-4

Newsletter Signup

For mothers everywhere

LIA

*L*ightning cracked the night sky as Lia slipped unnoticed out the back door of the bed-and-breakfast where she was staying in Key West. Steam rose from the pavement, and the air hung thick with moisture—an indication of more storms to come. She draped a navy silk scarf over her head and tied it under her chin to hide the oval-shaped scar that crept its way up the side of her neck to the edge of her jawbone. The sidewalks were empty. Foul weather had driven the throngs of tourists indoors. Gay laughter and loud music drifted from the nightclubs as she hurried down Duval Street toward her estranged husband's hotel.

With valet parking, a swim-up pool bar, and a private marina, the Buena Vista Resort was in a different league than her homey bed-and-breakfast with its country decor and clowder of cats lounging on the furniture and in windowsills.

How can Ricky afford even one night here, let alone an extended stay in the honeymoon suite? That tacky woman currently occupying his bed must be wealthy.

Last time Lia had seen him, nine months ago, her husband

was broke and on the run from vicious brutes willing to torture him if necessary to extract the money he owed them.

Entering the building through the main entrance, she lowered her head and stared at the floor, avoiding eye contact with the night clerk as she strolled past the check-in desk. Making her way to the bank of elevators, she ascended to the fifth floor. She emerged from the elevator into a dimly lit hallway with peeling wallpaper and worn carpet. Management clearly invested more effort and money maintaining the more visible areas of the hotel. She followed the arrows directing her to room 550. His door was ajar, and when she knocked, no one answered. She nudged the door open, crossed the threshold into the darkness, and groped for the light switch. Her fingers felt a sticky substance on the wall—this startled her. She took a step back, grabbing hold of the doorknob for support. She regained her balance and stared down at her hand. The sticky substance on her fingers was blood.

Heart pounding against her rib cage and sweat trickling down her back, she ventured farther into the room to the foot of the heart-shaped bed. She gasped and stifled a scream at the sight of her husband's mutilated body. A black-handled carving knife protruded from his chest, and there was blood everywhere—spattering the walls, saturating his khaki pants and striped golf shirt, and soaking the white bed linens beneath him. Backing slowly out of the room, she turned and fled in the opposite direction of the elevator, down the five flights of the emergency staircase. She burst through the exit door into the humid night and scurried up the gravel pathway toward the front entrance of the hotel.

ELLIE

The incessant pounding of hammer against nail set Ellie's nerves on edge. She couldn't escape the sounds of construction at home, where her building contractor was finishing up her kitchen renovation, or at work, where a separate crew labored to convert the old brick warehouse she'd recently purchased into an art gallery and studio. The only place Ellie found peace was at the elementary school where she volunteered two days a week—as much peace as any teacher could have among a group of eight spirited fourth graders. Popping two Tylenol for the headache brewing at the base of her skull, she communicated final instructions to her foreman before departing the building. She navigated the sidewalks of downtown Charleston, weaving her way through the crowds of women shopping the boutiques and lunching at the many artisan restaurants, on her way from Broad Street to the school.

Seven months ago, when she'd decided to make Charleston her permanent home, she'd convinced the principal at Peninsula Elementary to let her pilot an art program for underprivileged kids who expressed an interest in improving their drawing and painting skills. Her group consisted of six girls and two boys whose personalities differed greatly even though they were from the same socioeconomic background.

She arrived five minutes late for class to discover her students dancing around the room and singing into their fists to the sound of rap music blaring from one of the boys' iPhones. Their shoes bore holes and their clothes were worn, but they all carried a smartphone of some variety. When Terrell saw her watching them from the doorway, he snatched up his phone from the art table and clicked off the music.

"It's okay, Terrell. You may leave the music on as long as you keep it clean and turn the volume down." She entered the room and placed her bag on the chair behind the desk. "Music provides inspiration for our work. I listen to classical music when I paint, but every artist has their preference. Now"—Ellie clasped her hands together—"if we work really hard, I bet we can finish up our selfies today."

The children donned their smocks—men's button-down shirts Ellie had purchased at Goodwill—and spread themselves out at the two rectangular tables positioned in the center of the room. They'd devoted the last two classes to working on their self-portraits. In addition to handheld mirrors, she'd taken their photographs and printed copies for them to use as inspiration. The children had drawn their likenesses in pencil first and then gone over the lines with Sharpie markers.

"Today is the fun part. We're going to add color to our portraits." She set out trays of oil pastels on the tables. "I want you to give careful consideration to the colors you choose before you begin."

She circled the room, spending a few minutes with each child in turn. The critical eye with which they'd drawn their self-portraits both surprised and amused her. One boy's flat nose overpowered his face. A curtain of black hair shielded another girl's eyes and cheeks, leaving only her small mouth and pointy chin in view.

"Come now, Terrell," she said when she saw the oversize buckteeth in his drawing. "Your teeth aren't that big."

"Yes, they are. Look!" He curled his upper lip back to show her his teeth.

"I like your teeth," she said, elbow-bumping him. She doubted his parents had budgeted for orthodontia. "They make your face interesting. You take good care of those pearly whites and keep them brushed."

She approached the next child and peered over her shoulder at her selfie. Ruby, too, had exaggerated her most prominent facial feature. Instead of trying to re-create the trail of freckles that crossed the bridge of her nose, Ruby had covered her face in black dots the size of chicken pox.

"Someone got a little carried away with the marker." Ellie picked up a mirror on the table and held it in front of Ruby's face. "You have a fraction of the number of freckles that you've drawn."

When she placed a hand on Ruby's shoulder, the child flinched and drew away. "I'm sorry, honey. Did I hurt you?"

This talented fourth grader reminded Ellie of herself at that age, with an eagerness to learn and a pensive expression full of wisdom despite her youth. Most days her clear green eyes sparkled with enthusiasm, but today they glistened with unshed tears when she looked up at Ellie.

"I fell off my bike."

"Oh, you poor dear," Ellie said, tucking a strand of frizzy orange hair behind her ear. "I hope you didn't break anything. Do you need to see the nurse?"

"I'm fine." When Ruby tugged at the collar of her smock, Ellie saw angry bruise marks on her neck, which were far from "fine" in Ellie's mind.

She noticed the other children watching them and decided it best, for the child's sake, not to make a big deal about it in front of the others. She waited until after class to pull Ruby aside.

"Is everything okay at home, honey? You can trust me not to tell anyone if you have anything you want to talk about."

"No, ma'am," Ruby said, casting an anxious glance at the door. "Everything's fine."

Ellie handed the child one of her business cards. "Put this somewhere safe. All my numbers are on there. You can call me anytime you need to talk."

"Thank you." Ruby stuffed the card in the back pocket of her tattered jeans and hurried out of the room.

Ellie stood in the doorway, watching Ruby follow her classmates down the hall. Her shoulders were slumped, and her head hung low as though bearing the weight of the world. Ellie felt it in her gut: one of the other students was bullying her at school, or someone was mistreating her at home.

She tidied up the room, turned out the lights, and exited the building through the main entrance. The clean spring air cleared her head and pleased her senses with the fragrance of freshly cut grass and flowers in bloom as she strolled the half mile toward home. With Ruby at the forefront of her mind, she allowed her thoughts to drift back to the past, after her mother passed away and she'd gone to live with her father in California. She'd been a traumatized child of six, and the only way he'd been able to reach her was through art. He'd invited her into the private sanctum of his darkroom and supplied her with watercolors and a sketchbook. Perched on a stool in the corner, using one of his photographs as inspiration, she'd painted her first masterpiece.

Is Ruby using her art to escape a traumatic situation in her home?

She was two blocks from her house when Maddie, her housekeeper, pulled up beside her in her old-model Cutlass Supreme. She rolled the passenger window down. "Miss Ellie, I hope you don't mind me leaving early. The dentist gone see me 'bout that tooth that's been bothering me. I'll see you first thing in the morning."

Maddie had worked for the Pringle family for more than forty years. She'd helped Ellie through some difficult times when she was a child. Aside from a stepmother who was not the nurturing type, Maddie was the closest thing to a real mother she'd ever known.

"I hope all goes well with your tooth," Ellie said as she waved her on.

Ellie heard the whine of a circular saw as she rounded the corner from King Street onto South Battery Street. Making her way up the short driveway to the antebellum mansion she'd recently inherited from her grandmother, she nodded a greeting at the workman feeding a length of baseboard trim into the saw.

Ellie's architect husband, Julian, had researched the history of the house. Circa 1820, when the Georgian was built, the original kitchen had been housed in a separate building. When Ellie's great-great-grandparents bought the house in the early 1900s, they built a tiny kitchen off the dining room just big enough for their cook to prepare their meals. Judging from the antiquated appliances and worn-out flooring, subsequent Pringle family occupants had done little to modernize the kitchen in the hundred-plus years since then.

Julian was in the kitchen overseeing the installation of the crown molding when she entered through the back door. He'd done a commendable job of designing and managing the project.

"This looks nice," she said, staring up at the crown molding. "At the risk of sounding like a broken record, how long will it be before we finish?"

Her husband leaned over and kissed her cheek. "The painters will paint the trim and do touch-ups tomorrow. I received confirmation that the technicians are coming to install the countertops on Tuesday and the sinks Wednesday morning. If all goes as planned, we'll be eating our first home-cooked meal in three months on Wednesday night."

This brought a smile to her face. "Let's make it a party and invite Dad over."

"Invite the whole neighborhood," Julian said. "We have reason to celebrate."

She stepped back, admiring the coral-colored geometric wallpaper. "I spoke to Jackie this morning. She's having the table delivered on Monday."

Ellie had sold all her grandmother's belongings to an antiques dealer and junk collector. The heavy furniture, dark oriental rugs, and gloomy oil paintings were not her style. At Julian's insistence, she'd hired Jackie Hart of JSH Designs to decorate the rest of the house. The formal rooms now sported an eclectic mix of contemporary furnishings and Julian's handsome priceless antiques. The overall feel was stylishly elegant yet comfortable for a family with young children.

Pixie, her cocoa-colored Maltese, trotted into the kitchen, followed closely by Mills, Julian's golden retriever. She scooped Pixie up and gave Mills's head a rub.

"Where are the twins?"

"Upstairs." Julian pointed at the ceiling. "Finger painting with Becca."

After months of interviewing candidates, she'd finally found the ideal sitter to help take care of her three-year-old nieces. Much to her dismay, however, Ellie discovered she wouldn't be able to keep her for long. Having graduated from the College of Charleston the previous May, Becca had recently taken the LSAT and was applying to law schools for the fall. She was a temporary sitter for Ellie's temporary children. Nothing in Ellie's life at the moment felt permanent.

"Finger painting is my kind of fun. Here." She handed her dog to Julian. "I'll go see if I can offer some guidance."

"Don't ruin it for them, Ellie," Julian warned. "Let them express themselves without forcing your stylistic opinions on them."

Ellie and her father, Abbott, a retired wildlife photographer, were constantly on the lookout for signs of special hidden talents in the twins. It stood to reason that either Bella or Mya—or both —would have inherited the creative gene.

She was mounting the staircase when she heard the clanging of the front door knocker. "Julian!" she called back down the wide center hallway to her husband. "Will you please add fixing the doorbell to the punch list for the workmen?"

Julian's muffled voice responded, but she couldn't make out his words.

Opening the heavy front door, she was alarmed to see two uniformed police officers, a male and a female, standing with hats in hands on her piazza. Her heart beat in her throat as her mind raced through the whereabouts of her various family members. Had one of her loved ones been involved in an accident?

The girls and Julian are home. Has Maddie wrecked her car on the way to the dentist? What about Dad? What were his plans for the day?

And there was Katie, Julian's eight-year-old daughter who lived upstate with her mother in Spartanburg, South Carolina. She gripped the doorknob as she braced herself for bad news.

"Can I help you?"

From the looks of their youthful faces, Ellie doubted either officer was older than thirty.

"Are you Eleanor Pringle?" the female asked. Officer Grant, according to her name tag.

"I recently married. I'm Eleanor Hagood now. What can I do for you?"

The male officer, Officer Cain, took a step forward. "If we could have a moment of your time? We'd like to talk to you about your sister."

Ellie exhaled the breath she'd been holding at the mention of her sister. She felt relieved and then guilty for feeling relieved.

Has something bad happened to Lia?

"Of course. Come in." She stepped out of their way as they entered the house. She noticed Bella and Mya watching them from the top of the stairs and called up to the sitter, "Becca, will you please get the girls a snack and ask Julian to join me in his study?"

"Yes, ma'am." The babysitter took hold of the twins' hands as they started down the stairs.

"Let's go where we can talk in private," she said to the officers as she ushered them down the hall to the wood-paneled room that had once served as her grandmother's library. "Please, make yourselves comfortable." She gestured to the seating area in the center of the room. "My husband will be here in a minute."

Cain and Grant sat side by side in the center of the leather sofa, and Ellie took a seat in one of the upholstered chairs opposite them. Her decorator had brightened the room by using neutral tones in the patterned wool rug and in the fabrics on the furniture and drapes. The lamps, decorative pillows, and contemporary painting over the mantel added splashes of color in hues of blues and reds. Shortly after he moved in with her, Julian had claimed this space for his own. His drafting table now occupied one of two bright corners of the room, near the window.

The sound of Julian's hard-soled loafers on the oak floors in the hallway announced his arrival. "Officers," he said, shaking each of their hands before pulling up a chair close to Ellie.

Unable to contain herself any longer, Ellie said, "Tell me what's going on with my sister. Is she in some kind of trouble? I hope she hasn't been hurt in any way."

"Not your sister," Cain said. "Her husband. Ricky Bertram's body was discovered in the honeymoon suite at the Buena Vista Resort in Key West. He'd been stabbed multiple times with a boning knife, the kind fishermen use for cleaning fish."

A cold dread settled over Ellie's body as this information sunk in. Last she knew, her sister and her husband were estranged. "What does this have to do with my sister?"

Grant consulted her iPad. "Based on my conversation with the detective handling the case, your sister is wanted for questioning in his murder investigation. According to the hotel staff, your sister was staying at the hotel with him. She's disappeared, along with all her things."

"Do you know for certain it was my sister? The last time I saw her, Lia and her husband were having marital problems."

"They were registered as 'Mr. and Mrs. Bertram.' And the woman staying with Ricky matches your sister's description." Once again, Grant looked down at her iPad. "Tall and thin, with dark hair and eyes."

"When is the last time either of you heard from Lia Bertram?" Officer Cain asked.

"Seven months ago," Julian answered.

"My sister and I aren't close," Ellie said. "I can tell you what I know about her in three minutes or less."

"We'd like to hear it, if you think it'll help the case," Grant said.

"Okay then." Ellie sat up straighter in her chair. "We were separated when we were young, too young to remember, in fact. Lia and I are twins, but I never knew she existed until I inherited this house from my grandmother and moved to Charleston in September of last year. I found out about my sister by reading old journals of my mother's that I came across in the attic." She saw the confused expression on Cain's face and added, "I know what you're thinking, officer. How can a woman with fair skin, green eyes, and auburn hair like me be twins with a woman with such dark features. We're fraternal twins. We look nothing alike."

"Thanks for the clarification," he said, and nodded. "Please continue."

"After our discovery, as you can imagine, my father and I immediately went to Georgia looking for her. Little did we—"

"Wait a minute," Grant said. "Are you saying your father didn't know about your twin sister, either?"

Ellie shook her head. "For personal reasons, my mother and grandmother chose to keep her existence a secret. That part of the story is long, Officer. And I don't see how it's relevant to your case."

Grant started to object, but Cain shot her a look. "We'll skip it for now and circle back later if need be."

Ellie glanced at Julian, who placed his hand over hers for support. "As I was saying, we had no idea we were walking into a hornet's nest of a mess in Decatur, Georgia. Ricky had borrowed money from a questionable source to pay off his gambling debts. When this questionable source sent his goons to collect his money, Ricky disappeared, leaving Lia with only thirty dollars in their joint bank account. With Ricky out of the picture, the goons started threatening Lia. That's when we showed up. Dad and I insisted she and her three-year-old daughters—who are also fraternal twins—come back to Charleston with us. I was able to convince Lia to stay only for a couple of days. She seemed agitated, like something was bothering her, although she never confided in me about what. I gave her some money, quite a lot of it, to help her get back on her feet. She left town in the middle of the night, and I haven't heard from her since."

Grant knitted her eyebrows. "And this was when?"

"At the end of September, this past year." The officer's jaw dropped open, and Ellie added, "I know what you're thinking, Officer Grant. What kind of mother leaves her toddlers in a virtual stranger's care for seven months? I've been trying to find her. I've spoken to the police in Decatur a number of times. I assume that's how you knew to contact me."

"That's correct," Grant said with an affirmative nod of his head. "The detective in Key West contacted by the police in Decatur, who suggested we reach out to you."

"Did your sister leave any kind of note or forwarding address?" Cain asked.

Ellie told them about the letter Lia had left, proclaiming

herself an unfit mother, and the text message her father had read by accident on Lia's phone from someone she'd stored in her contacts as Lover Boy.

"She was planning to meet her Lover Boy, but we don't know where. Ricky could've been that Lover Boy for all we know. We never got a chance to ask Lia before she took off."

Julian moved to the edge of his seat. "And you're sure the deceased is Ricky Bertram? Has anyone identified the body?"

"According to the Georgia driver's license they found in his wallet, the victim is Richard Bertram of Cherry Blossom Lane in Decatur, Georgia. Detective Hamlin informed me that Ricky's brother is on his way to Key West as we speak to claim the body." Grant clicked a button on her iPad, and the screen went dark. "We'll be in touch if we have additional questions." She handed Ellie a business card and stood to leave. "In the meantime, if you hear from your sister, be sure to let us know."

ELLIE

*E*llie called her father as soon as the police officers left. He lived around the corner in Julian's old converted carriage house and arrived on her piazza within minutes.

Bella clasped onto his right leg while Mya leaped into his arms and wrapped her tiny hands around his neck. "GoPa! Did you bring us a surprise?"

No one knew where the twins came up with their nickname for their grandfather, but everyone agreed it suited him. Abbott was a hip grandfather who was always on the go.

"Let me see." Shifting Mya to his other arm, he dug into his right pocket and produced two bouncy rubber balls the size of gumballs. "Looka here. Wonder how these got in my pocket."

Mya tried to grab the balls, but Abbott held them away from her. "Not in the house. You might break one of your Aunt Ellie's pretty things." He eyed the antique Turkish runner in the center hallway. "Looks to me like someone's made a purchase since I was last here three days ago."

"The rug is part of an installment Jackie delivered yesterday," Ellie explained. "You'll love what's she's done in the living room. I'll show you everything later."

Ellie noticed Becca standing off to the side, as though waiting for the right opportunity to interrupt. The young woman's manners were impeccable. She had a soft-spoken, graceful ease about her that Ellie found endearing. The twins simply adored her, which made Ellie feel less guilty about paying a babysitter to stay with them three days a week. As much as Ellie wanted to be a mother, she wasn't ready to give up her career as an artist. Since the twins had come to live with her, she'd developed a newfound respect for modern working women who juggled both family and career.

Ellie glanced at the grandfather clock down the hall. It was only five thirty, and Becca usually stayed until six. "Do you need to leave early today?"

Becca bobbed her strawberry-blonde head. With pale blue eyes and sun-kissed cheeks, she was pretty in a wholesome way. "The wind has kicked up. If you don't mind, I'd like to get some practice in before the regatta this weekend."

"Then what are you waiting for? Go!" Ellie held the front door open for the sitter. "Have fun and be careful. We'll see you in the morning."

Ellie closed the door behind Becca and turned to the twins. "Say, girls, let's go out to the garden so you can play with your balls."

"Yay!" the twins cried. They ran ahead of them, down the hall, through the Florida room Ellie used as an art studio, and out the french doors to the walled backyard.

"Go get 'em, girls!" Abbott said as he bounced the rubber balls off the bluestone terrace into the yard.

With shrieks of laughter, the girls went chasing after the balls.

"Where's Julian?" Abbott asked.

"In the kitchen, giving the workmen their last instructions for the day. He'll be out in a minute. Let's sit down." She motioned toward a round umbrellaed table.

When they were seated across from each other, Abbott said,

"I'm having a hard time grasping what you told me on the phone. Do you seriously think Lia is capable of murdering her husband?"

Ellie paused before answering. "I'm not sure. I don't think either of us knows Lia well enough to make that judgment. During the two days we spent with her last fall, she was pretty difficult. I'd even go so far as to say her attitude toward us was hostile."

"But her letter explained her behavior. She was struggling with the decision to leave the girls in your care."

"But also in that letter, she declared herself mentally unstable."

A solemn expression crossed his face. "I guess that makes her a candidate for murder suspect. I barely know her, but I'm still her father. I owe it to her to give her the benefit of the doubt until we can find out more."

"I would expect nothing less from you, Daddy." Her father was the most scrupulous person she'd ever met. "I'm sure you're right anyway. Lia might be selfish and insincere and difficult to get along with, but I don't think she's a murderer. Ricky owed some bad men a lot of money. My guess is those men finally caught up to him."

Julian appeared on the terrace with a tray of sweet tea. He handed each of them a glass and sat down between them. "So . . . how do we proceed?"

"This is the closest we've come to finding Lia," Ellie said, pressing her cool glass against her warm cheek. "I have no choice but to go to Key West."

Julian cut his eyes at her. "Not alone, you're not."

"Julian's right." Abbott glanced at the girls to make sure they were out of earshot. He leaned across the table and lowered his voice. "If she did kill her husband, you could be walking into a dangerous situation. What will you do if you find her, anyway? Drag her back to Charleston?"

"I have to try, Dad. I need to know what Lia's intentions are concerning Bella and Mya. It's unfair of her to expect me to take care of her children indefinitely. Don't get me wrong. I'm happy to do it. I love them as much as you do. But this arrangement is making me an emotional basket case. Every morning when I wake up, I fear that it will be the day Lia comes for the girls."

"I know it's hard on you, sweetheart," Abbott said. "I've felt that way a few hundred times myself."

"Julian and I have made a home for them here." Ellie's eyes traveled across the yard to the girls. "Look at them. They're happy and well adjusted. They've stopped asking about their mommy and daddy. It will tear my heart out if Lia takes them away. I understand they're her children, and she has every right to take them whenever and wherever she chooses, but I question whether it's in the girls' best interest to be with their biological mother if she's unstable."

"We don't know for certain that she's unsta—"

Ellie silenced her father with an arched eyebrow. "And we don't know for certain she wasn't involved in her husband's murder either," Ellie said. "No mother in her right mind leaves her children with a woman she barely knows—even if she is her sister—for seven months without so much as a phone call."

They sat in silence while they watched the girls attempt to toss the tiny ball back and forth to each other. "Selfishly, I'd like to see them stay in Charleston," Abbott said. "But I worry that if you force Lia's hand, she'll take them away out of spite."

Ellie rested her hand on her husband's forearm. "If Lia ever plans on reclaiming them, it's better emotionally for Julian and me if it happens now rather than ten years from now. We didn't tell you, Dad, but we consulted an attorney regarding the matter. We've already petitioned for legal guardianship, the first step toward legally adopting them. We need to make every effort to find the girls' parents before we can move forward with the adoption. We had him draw up adoption papers so that we will be prepared on the off chance that Lia comes back for more money and is willing to sign over permanent custody to us in exchange."

Abbott's mouth fell open. "You're going to barter with your sister for custody of the twins?"

Ellie shrugged. "Whatever it takes, Dad. Julian and I have discussed this at length with each other and our attorney. We are all in agreement."

"What's to stop her from trying to claim them down the road?" Abbott asked.

"There's a provision in the adoption papers preventing it," Julian said.

"And what's going to stop her from contesting it?" Abbott asked.

"She can try all day long," Julian said. "No judge in his right mind will give children back to a woman who signed over custody of her children in exchange for money."

Abbott gulped his tea. "Let me get this straight. You're going to Key West with these papers, hoping she'll sign them in exchange for a check?"

"No, Dad. You've got it all wrong. I'm not going to Key West to bait my sister. My main purpose in taking this trip is to locate her, determine her state of mind, and find out her plans for the future. We would've gone to see her months ago, but we had no idea where to find her until today. I'll have the papers on hand, though, in case that future doesn't include the twins."

Julian said, "Our attorney believes that, based on the letter Lia left Ellie, we won't have any trouble with the adoption. But your daughter, being the overly considerate, amazing woman I married, would like to make certain this is what Lia wants."

Abbott looked back and forth between Ellie and Julian. "I can see you've given this a lot of thought." He sighed. "I trust you know best in this situation. I'll stay here with the girls while you're gone."

A sense of calm settled over Ellie.

Maybe everything will turn out all right after all.

"Are you sure, Dad? I hate to ask you to do that with the house in such a mess and the makeshift kitchen."

He dismissed her concern with a sweeping hand gesture. "We can eat at my house if we choose. We'll be fine."

"Becca and Maddie will be here tomorrow," Ellie said. "Becca is sailing in a regatta on Saturday, but I can have Maddie come in over the weekend if need be."

Abbott placed his hand over hers and squeezed. "Don't worry, honey. We'll work it out. I promise we'll be fine."

Ellie fell back in her chair and then sat up straight. "Wait! I thought Tracey was coming this weekend." Her father had been in a relationship with his current girlfriend for several months when he decided to move from DC to Charleston. She'd been worried for some time their romance wouldn't survive the commute.

A rubber ball soared through the air toward them. Abbott caught it and bounced it back to the twins. "I'm sorry to say she canceled on me again. She has a crisis at work. It's for the best. We talked for a long time the other night and agreed things weren't going to work out for us."

"That's a bummer, Dad." As much as her father was enamored by Charleston, Ellie hated the idea of him having to experience it alone. With his dark handsome looks and his fun-loving personality, he was a catch for any woman his age. "Maybe you'll find a Charlestonian who is equally charming."

A mischievous smile played on his lips. "As it so happens, I may have already found that someone."

Ellie planted her elbows on the table and stretched across the table toward him. "Do tell, Dad."

Abbott chuckled. "There's not much to tell yet. She's a photographer. Our paths have crossed a couple of times on our pursuit of the quintessential shot."

Ellie's fingers flew to her lips as she bit back laughter. "Sounds like a match made in heaven."

"What's her name?" Julian asked. "I may know her."

Ellie rolled her eyes. "I'm sure you do. You know everyone else in this town."

"Her name is Lacey," Abbott said. "Lacey Sinkler."

Julian grinned. "She's my first cousin. Her mother is my mother's older sister. Lacey used to babysit for me when I was a kid."

Ellie threw her hands in the air. "Why am I not surprised?"

"I can see how the two of you might hit it off," Julian said. "Lacey loves bird-watching as much as you do. Have you asked her out yet?"

"Not yet. But I will soon, now that my relationship with Tracey is officially over."

"Speaking of photography, how's your exhibit coming? This is your first series in a long time. I know how hard you've been working on it and want to get it right. The gallery is opening in a month. I hope our trip to Key West doesn't interfere with your work schedule."

"On the contrary. I'm planning to photograph the Angel Oak Tree on Saturday," he said, referring to the ancient live oak on Johns Island, a thirty-minute drive south of Charleston. "I'll take the girls with me. They'll get a kick out of seeing it."

"Seriously, Dad? The Angel Oak Tree? Isn't that a little unconventional for you? That tree has been photographed at least a gazillion times."

"Not by me," he said, brushing an imaginary speck of lint off his shoulder.

Ellie shook her head. "A tree is a tree is a tree."

Julian stood up from the table. "I'm taking your dad's side this time. You've never seen the Angel Oak. It's quite spectacular." He kissed the top of her head. "I'll go get my laptop, so we can book our flights." He left the table and disappeared inside.

Ellie stuck her tongue out at Abbott. "You can wipe the smirk off your face. Maybe I'll paint the Angel Tree."

With eyebrows raised, he stared at her over the rim of his sweet tea glass. "If you're nice to me, I'll let you have one of my photographs to paint over."

"Ha ha. Aren't you the funny guy?"

"Come chase us, GoPa," the twins called from the yard in unison.

Abbott pushed back from the table abruptly. "You want the big furry monster to chase you, do you? Well, here he comes!" With legs stiff and arms flailing above his head, he went after the twins.

Ellie sipped her tea while she watched the show.

Amid the girls' squeals of delight, he chased them in circles around the small yard, almost catching them three times before finally stumbling and falling. He got to his knees and crawled on all fours. "I'm getting weak. Feed me, please. I need food." He collapsed on the ground, and they climbed on top of him. "I'll die if you don't feed me."

Julian returned to the terrace with his computer. "I guess we'd better order some dinner."

"Girls, ask the monster what he wants for dinner," Ellie called.

"What do you want for dinner, GoPa?"

"Anything but pizza. We've eaten so much pizza since these renovations started, we're all gonna turn into pepperonis and sausage balls."

The twins giggled. "You're so funny, GoPa!" Bella said.

He removed the twins from his torso and slowly got up. "I'm getting too old for this, girls. Y'all run along and play and let the poor monster rest for a minute."

Julian's fingers tapped away at the keyboard. "Delta has a flight leaving at seven tomorrow morning. Is that too early?"

"That depends on Dad," Ellie said. "But I'd like to get there as soon as possible."

"Fine by me," Abbott said, reclaiming his seat at the table. "I'll spend the night tonight, so I'll be here with the twins when you leave in the morning."

"Should I book a return now?" Julian asked.

"Why don't you keep the return open for now?" Abbott suggested. "Stay as long as you like. You two never got to take a honeymoon. You deserve some time alone together."

"I appreciate the offer, but there's no way Mr. Architect"— she squeezed Julian's shoulder—"will abandon his project in the final critical stages. The countertops are coming on Tuesday and the sinks on Wednesday."

"Oh no, you don't." Julian snapped his computer shut and sat back in his chair. "You're in the driver's seat on this trip, Ellie. We'll come back when you're ready."

"I admit the idea of a little fun in the sun is appealing, but now is not the right time for a vacation. My goal is to find Lia, have her sign the papers, and get back home as soon as possible."

When a rubber ball whizzed past Ellie's head, Abbott grabbed it out of the air before it knocked over his tea glass. "Come here, you two," he called to the girls. They raced to his side. "How would you like for GoPa to stay with you for a few days while Aunt Ellie and Uncle Julian go out of town on business?"

"Really? Will you?" They bounced up and down on their tippy-toes.

"Really, I will!" Abbott placed a hand on top of each of their heads, holding them down until they squirmed. "We can stay up late watching TV and eating ice cream!"

Ellie shot him a death glare. "Don't you dare!"

Abbott faked a dejected look. "All right. We'll abide by the rules. But that doesn't mean we can't still have fun."

Julian stood and stretched. "Girls, why don't the three of us go pick up some dinner while GoPa goes home to pack and Aunt Ellie searches for her bikini?"

"Bikini, hell," Ellie said under her breath. "I'm traveling light. The only items I'm packing in my suitcase are a pair of shorts, two T-shirts, and the adoption papers."

ELLIE

*E*llie spent longer than usual with the girls at bedtime. They wanted extra time in the bathtub, and afterward, selected a large stack of books from the shelves in their playroom adjoining their bedroom for her to read. She hated the idea of leaving them for Florida. She had complete faith in her father's ability to take care of them, but what if one of them got sick or fell and broke a bone? What if something bad happened to her father during the night and the girls were left all by themselves? What if someone kidnapped them? What if Lia wasn't in Key West but in Charleston, lurking in the shadows of the live oak trees in the park across the street? Was this how all parents felt when they traveled without their children? Or was her mind conjuring up these irrational fears as a result of the constant threat that Lia would one day show up and take the girls away? How would Ellie cope then? When her parental responsibilities were terminated after seven long months. When Lia whisked the girls off to some unknown place and she never had contact with them again. She would no longer have control over any aspect of their lives. Would she ever be able to let go, or would the worry intensify to the point it drove her completely insane?

She brewed a cup of chamomile tea and returned to the terrace. She relaxed on the chaise lounge and stared up at the stars. The moonlight beamed down on the magnolia tree in the far back corner of the yard. When she'd lived here as a child, the tree had provided shelter from the abuse she suffered from her grandmother and an escape from the sorrow of watching her mother die. Closing her eyes, she thought back to all the changes that had taken place in her life since she'd inherited the property and moved to Charleston nine months ago. The things Ellie learned from her mother's journals unleashed memories of traumatic events that her subconscious had held captive since her childhood. The most astonishing of her revelations was the little girl with dark hair and eyes who turned out to be her twin sister.

Abbott had come to Charleston to help search for Lia and never returned to his home in Washington, DC. Like Ellie, he fell in love with his granddaughters and was enamored with the Lowcountry—the milder climate, friendly folks, and delectable cuisine served at the high-end restaurants and outdoor cafés. He worked remotely for a while before exchanging his position as creative vice president for a part-time consulting position at *National Geographic*.

Ellie met Julian during her first week in Charleston. After a whirlwind romance, they got married two days before Christmas while Julian's daughter was visiting over her winter break. The chapel at Saint Philip's Church was decked for the holidays in fresh greens and red poinsettias. The small group of attendees, made up mostly of Julian's friends, admired the elegant bride— dressed in a winter-white suit with her auburn hair styled into a sleek chignon—as the proud father walked her down the aisle. The twins and Katie were her only attendants, three little angels in white velvet dresses with red-satin sashes. Ellie and Julian hosted a wedding brunch, catered by Charleston's most sought-after caterer, Heidi Butler, for family and friends at Julian's carriage house on Church Street. The bride and groom opted not to go on a honeymoon but to spend Christmas Day and the week afterward with the girls. The twins idolized Katie and she, in turn, doted on them. Julian and Ellie took their small family on a few outings, but mostly they camped out by the fire, watching holiday movies and roasting marshmallows on wire coat hangers in the fireplace. It was the happiest time of Ellie's life, and they were sad to see Katie return to her mother in Spartanburg after New Year's.

They'd seen Katie only three times since Christmas. While Julian's custody agreement stipulated twice-a-month visits, Katie's extracurricular activities—her basketball league games during the winter months and her soccer team tournaments in the spring—had forced her to cancel their scheduled weekends. Julian was growing tired of being patient, and Ellie had become suspicious of the situation. During her last visit over Easter, Katie had seemed unusually subdued and somewhat hostile toward Ellie. She worried her husband's ex-wife was filling her daughter's head with untruths about her father's new wife. Ellie had encouraged Julian to keep a journal of the missed weekends, unreturned phone messages, and other matters concerning Katie in the event he needed to present them to a judge down the road.

With Ellie's biological clock running out of time, she and Julian had agreed to start a family soon after the wedding. They prepared themselves for fertility challenges, but were pleasantly surprised when she got pregnant the second month. Her doctor warned her of the risks associated with first-time pregnancies for women over forty, but Ellie remained cautiously optimistic. Her morning sickness continued throughout the day, which Dr. Gillespie agreed was a positive sign.

Ellie heard the french door open behind her and the scratching of the dogs' nails as they scrambled across the bluestone terrace. Julian nudged Ellie to move over and snuggled up beside her on the lounge chair. "I noticed you ate a lot of dinner. You must be feeling better today."

"I am feeling better, and Mexican was a pleasant change from pizza. Just as the doctors promised would happen at the beginning of the second trimester." She nestled into him. "I can't wait to tell Dad about the baby. He'll be ecstatic."

"Why not tell him tonight?"

"He's already gone to bed. I'll tell him when we get back from Florida. He's worried enough about us making this trip. He doesn't need to fret about my high-risk pregnancy."

Julian pressed his hand against her still-flat tummy. "And how's the little one today?"

"He's fine." For Julian's sake, because he was already surrounded by females, Ellie was hoping for a boy. "But you can guess again if you think I'm putting this bloated body in a bikini."

He nibbled at her neck. "I'll settle for the one-piece, as long as it's the sexy pink number that's cut way down in the back."

She elbowed him in the ribs. "This is not a pleasure trip, Julian. We're going to Key West for one thing and one thing only."

"You heard your father. We never got our honeymoon. Surely we can make time for at least one moonlit swim."

She envisioned their bodies entwined in a secluded swimming pool with palm trees swaying overhead. "Well . . . maybe just one."

"Hmm." His hand moved from her belly to her breast. "I can feel the tropical breeze already."

She swatted his hand away. "This is serious, Julian. What if we don't find Lia? What happens then?"

"We'll put pressure on Tyler to expedite the legal guardianship so we can move forward with adoption proceedings." Tyler Burke was the attorney they'd hired to consult with them about their case.

Ellie sighed. "I know it's unrealistic of me to want Lia's blessing on the adoption."

"She already gave you her blessing. In writing, no less."

"That may be true, but I'm not convinced her letter will hold up in court if she gets herself a good attorney. He'll make the case that she was going through a difficult time. And she was. She was under a great deal of stress. Her husband had gambled away all their money and left her to deal with the fallout from his bad decisions. She had plenty of reason to freak out. I would've too, under those circumstances. But Bella and Mya are *her* daughters. I think it's only fair to give her another chance before we move forward. I would want someone to do the same for me if the situation were reversed. If, on the other hand, we find Lia and she's strung out on crack cocaine . . . well, then that's a different scenario entirely."

"Are you prepared for her to take the girls back?"

Ellie craned her neck so she could see his face. "No more than you are. But if it's going to happen, I'd rather it be now, when I'm anticipating it to happen, than out of the blue ten years from now."

He rolled onto his back and placed his hand behind his head. "I hear what you're saying, and I'm willing to play it your way for now. But if we don't find Lia in Key West, I'm going to insist we petition the court for custody. We have Lia's letter as evidence. If you ask me, the petition is simply a formality. The tone and wording of the letter implies she won't be coming back anytime soon. She admits that she's not mentally stable and is a dangerous threat to her children. She talks about how Abbott will be a supportive presence in the girls' lives, and she tells you not to try and find her. We have all this in Lia's handwriting. We'll wrap the case up so tight she won't be able to reclaim those children if and when she ever resurfaces."

"I wish I felt as confident as you sound." She pushed herself to a sitting position and swung her legs over the side of the chair. "I'm going to bed. We have a long day ahead of us tomorrow."

ELLIE

The plane trip from Charleston to Key West via Atlanta was uneventful. Ellie and Julian took a taxi from the airport directly to the Buena Vista Resort in the heart of downtown, arriving hours too early for check-in. They left their bags with the front desk clerk, who promised to have them delivered to their room as soon as one became available.

After they finished with the paperwork, Ellie asked to speak with the hotel manager. "I have a personal issue I need to discuss. Is he or she around?"

"I believe so. Let me check." The young Hispanic woman disappeared into the back office and returned with a heavyset bald man who introduced himself as Fred Porter.

Ellie extended her hand. "I'm looking for my sister, Lia, Mr. Porter. Her husband, Ricky Bertram, was murdered in your hotel two nights ago."

A pained expression crossed his face as he glanced around to see if any hotel guests were listening. "Why don't we step down here, where we can speak in private?" The desk clerk motioned them to the end of the check-in counter. "I'm not sure how I can help, Mrs. Hagood. I already told the detectives everything I know."

"My sister and her husband were having marital problems, Mr. Porter. I know the woman you described to the police matches Lia's description, but you can understand why I need to make certain it was her." Ellie removed her cell phone from her bag and accessed the photograph of Lia her father had taken during their brief time together the previous fall. "She wears turtlenecks most of the time, to cover a burn scar on her neck."

Porter took the phone from Ellie and studied the picture carefully. He jabbed his finger at the screen and shook his head. "This is not the same woman. They are similar in looks, with dark hair and eyes, but the woman staying here with Mr. Bertram wore tight-fitting clothing that showed off her figure. And she had a figure, too, if you know what I mean. She paraded through the lobby several times in her bathing suit, a tiny little bikini that . . ." He shook his head as he remembered the sight of the woman in the bikini. "Wow."

"How long did they stay here?" Julian asked.

"Two weeks and three days," Porter said. "I know this, because the police asked the same question."

Ellie's mouth fell open. "I find that hard to believe, since my brother-in-law was broke," she said, even though that tidbit of information was none of Porter's business. "What's the nightly rate?"

"Four hundred and fifty dollars," Porter said. "Perhaps his girlfriend was footing the bill."

"Did you not think that unusual?" Ellie asked. "Most honeymoons only last a week."

"This is Key West, Mrs. Hagood. Nothing that happens here surprises me."

She tapped on the phone with her fingernail. "Have you ever seen this woman?"

He glanced once more at the picture and then handed Ellie

her phone. "If I have, I don't remember. A lot of people come in and out of this hotel every day."

She dropped her phone in her bag. "Is there anything else you can tell me about the woman staying here with Ricky, other than the shape of her body and the color of her hair? She may know something of my sister's whereabouts."

"Actually . . ." He held up his index finger. "Wait one minute." He disappeared into the back office and returned with a computer printout bearing the image of a striking brunette. "This photograph was taken from our security surveillance video. The image is kinda grainy, but you can get a general idea of what she looks like. I hope you find her, although I suspect she's long gone from here by now. The police are hot on her trail."

Ellie looked down at the woman, who bore a striking resemblance to her sister. "How did the couple seem when they were together? Did you or any of your guests witness anything out of the ordinary?"

He thought about it a minute before responding, "Nope."

"No one reported loud arguing coming from their room?"

He shook his head. "Sorry. They seemed very much in love, like normal honeymooners, which is why I didn't question their extended stay."

"WHAT NOW?" Julian asked as they stood outside the entrance to the hotel.

"First, we eat. I'm starving." Ellie took off down the hotel's driveway toward Duval Street.

Julian caught up with her and stepped in line beside her. "Do you have any idea where you're going?"

"Not really. I figured we'd wing it with a little help from Yelp." She retrieved the phone from her bag and accessed the app. "What're you in the mood for: seafood or burgers?"

31

"Is that a serious question? We can't come to Key West and not eat seafood." He took her phone and after a brief perusal of Yelp said, "Let's hit DJ's Clam Shack. Reviews are good, and it's right up the road a couple of blocks." He handed the phone back to her.

"After we eat, before we go to the police station, I'd like to stop in at some of the bed-and-breakfasts around here and show them Lia's photograph on the off chance she's in the area."

"You're in charge, honey. But don't get your hopes up. You heard the hotel manager. The woman staying at the Buena Vista with Ricky was not Lia."

Ellie increased her pace. "That doesn't mean she's not in Key West. I have this odd feeling she's nearby. Maybe it's wishful thinking. Maybe it's that weird thing twins share that enables them to sense each other's presence."

"Have you ever experienced this extrasensory perception before where Lia is concerned?"

"Not hardly. I barely know her."

Julian chuckled. "That's what I thought."

"I don't even know why I said that. I can't think straight on an empty stomach." Her mouth watered at the thought of food. "Maybe Lia was stalking her husband *and* this mystery woman."

"That's pretty far-fetched, babe." He took her by the arm and increased his pace. "Come on. We need to get you some food to straighten out your thinking."

The sidewalks grew more crowded after they crossed Truman Avenue. Hand in hand, they meandered through the throng of tourists as they made their way up Duval Street to DJ's Clam Shack. They were awarded their choice of seating—a table for two at the front of the small patio alongside the sidewalk—having arrived ahead of the lunch crowd. Julian asked for a Sam Adams and Ellie sweet tea. They then ordered conch fritters, clam strips, and a lobster roll to share. As soon as the order was served, Ellie cut the lobster roll in half and took a big bite.

"This is so good, I might have to order another one—all for myself." She took a second bite and wiped her lips. "You have no idea how happy I am to have my appetite back after three months of feeling nauseous. I literally want to eat everything in sight." She reached for the basket of clam strips and stuffed two in her mouth.

Julian smiled. "Go for it! You're eating for two, after all."

Ellie wadded up a napkin and tossed it at him. "Some help you are. With your attitude, I'll gain two hundred pounds by the time the baby comes. It's your job to help me control my diet."

"For once in your life, you don't have to worry about your diet. You've barely eaten a thing in three months. You can splurge a little now. Listen to your body. If you're hungry, eat." He popped a conch fritter into her mouth.

"But I should be eating healthy, not all this fried seafood," she said, waving her hand at the food baskets.

"It won't hurt the baby if you indulge every now and then. But if it makes you feel better, we'll eat grilled seafood for dinner tonight."

"Dinner is a long time off. We have a lot of work ahead of us this afternoon."

While they finished eating, she googled bed-and-breakfasts in Key West and set her iPhone on the table in front of them. They studied the TripAdvisor listings and decided which area to search first.

Ellie was gathering up their trash when a woman window-shopping in the gift store on the other side of the street caught her eye. She wore her dark hair piled on top of her head, and large-framed sunglasses covered much of her face. The hotel manager had mentioned that the female staying with Ricky wore skimpy clothes. You couldn't get much skimpier than the woman's white sundress, cut low enough to reveal a tattoo at the small of her back.

"Don't look now, Julian, but I think that's Ricky's mystery woman on the other side of the street."

Julian drained the rest of his beer as he studied the woman. "It looks like her. Then again, I'm sure there are hundreds of women in Key West who match her description."

"What'd we do? We can't just let her get away."

He set his empty beer bottle on the table. "You stay here while I see what I can find out."

"Be careful." As her husband cut through the line of patrons waiting for a table and moseyed across the street, she watched his every step. He casually approached the woman and spoke to her. Shaking her head, she backed away from him, turned, and took off running in the opposite direction.

Bingo! Ellie thought. *She wouldn't be running unless she had something to hide.*

Ellie dumped their trash in a nearby garbage can, gathered their belongings, and hurried out of the restaurant. On the sidewalk out front, she stood on her tiptoes and shielded her eyes from the sun as she searched over the sea of bobbing heads. She caught a glimpse of Julian's brown hair at the end of the block, just before he disappeared into the crowd. With her hand gripping her cell phone, Ellie paced back and forth in front of DJ's Clam Shack until he returned a few minutes later. Sweat dripped from his face, and the armpits of his navy golf shirt were soaked through.

"I'm sorry, honey. She got away." He removed her cardigan from her straw tote bag and wiped the sweat from his face.

"What did you say to her?" Ellie asked.

"I asked her if she by any chance knew Lia Bertram."

Ellie grabbed a handful of her husband's sweaty shirt and dragged him down the sidewalk, back toward their hotel. "Forget the bed-and-breakfasts for now. We need to talk to Detective Hamlin."

LIA

*L*ia was strolling down Duval Street, minding her own business, when she spotted her sister seated at a table on the patio at DJ's Clam Shack across the street. She darted into a nearby gift shop and lost herself among the aisles of cheap souvenirs, beach towels, and sunscreen. She pulled her sun hat low enough to hide her face and adjusted the floral scarf around her neck. When she deemed it safe, she made her way back to the front of the store so she could observe her sister from behind the mannequin in the window.

"Ellie Darling" took a bite of her lobster roll and dabbed her lips with her napkin.

Such a lady, my sister.

The sun cast a golden glow on Ellie's auburn hair, creating a halo effect, like an angel.

How can a woman I've known for such a short time get under my skin so easily? If only Ellie weren't so perfect.

Twin sisters: one the ideal daughter, wife, and mother; the other flawed to the bone.

Would our personalities have differed so greatly if we'd been identical twins instead of fraternal?

Lia had been relieved, at first, when her long-lost sister and father showed up at her door in the midst of the biggest crisis of her life.

Convenient for me. Not so much for them.

They'd insinuated themselves into her life, insisting Lia let them take care of her and the twins. But once Ellie had gotten to know Lia, once she'd realized that Lia lacked any moral fortitude, Ellie had reneged on her offer to share half of her inheritance from their grandmother.

It was with a heavy heart that Lia had left her daughters in her sister's care. She loved Bella and Mya enough to want the best for them, even if the best wasn't her. She'd made a mess of her marriage and had an affair with another man. Ellie had practically begged Lia to leave the girls with her while she sorted out her life. And, eager to be in the arms of her lover, Lia had taken the money her sister had offered and gone off to find herself. And she'd made a monumental discovery—the revelation that she no longer wanted to be a mother.

What was Ellie Darling doing in Key West, anyway? Unless the police had contacted her about Ricky's death and warned her to be on the lookout for her dangerous twin sister, the murderer. She imagined Eleanor jumping on the next plane to Key West, eager to be a character witness for the defense and provide testimony regarding her twin's questionable morals. Sending her to prison for life would grant Ellie permanent custody of the twins. She and Julian and the twins could live out their perfect little lives in their big mansion on the most prestigious street in Charleston.

Not so fast, Ellie Darling! Part of that mansion rightfully belongs to me.

She slipped out of the gift shop and stepped in line with a group of tourists heading west on Duval Street, away from her sister. She knew she needed to leave Key West as soon as possible

—before the police or her sister found her. If only she knew where to go.

She'd hopped on the first bus to Key West six days ago when she received the first text from Ricky. She'd been suspicious of his sudden interest in discussing their future. Ricky was cautious to a fault, always nagging her about keeping their doors locked and never taking her eyes off the children while out shopping. With his unpaid balance to the loan sharks, Ricky would've understood the danger in summoning his estranged wife to Key West. Out of curiosity, she'd come to town anyway. And spent the days leading up to his murder spying on him from behind the potted plants in the hotel lobby. Someone had framed her for Ricky's murder. Maybe the goons were still following her. Maybe her presence in town had gotten Ricky killed. But Lia suspected the trashy woman he was currently sleeping with had something to do with his murder. Whichever of them was the guilty party, Lia had no intention of taking the fall.

Ricky and Lia's marriage had been on the rocks long before the twins were born—they would turn four on the twenty-fourth of this month. She was all too aware of her husband's extramarital activities.

Three months before Ricky split town, she had been at a bar in downtown Atlanta, looking for a man to show her some attention. That was the night she met Justin Palmer. They hooked up a couple of times during his brief stay in Atlanta, and continued to text and talk daily after he left. He offered comfort and support when her husband abandoned her and a shoulder to cry on while she sorted out her life. Their attraction was intense. Before they met, Justin's drinking problem had led to the loss of his wife, his job, and his house—in that order. He'd been in Atlanta for a job interview, but didn't get that job. Or any of the other dozen he'd applied for while they were together. Despite his professional shortcomings, Justin was a blast to hang out with, and he helped her forget her troubles.

They went on a nine-month bender, bouncing around the country from one exciting city to the next. They made love on the sandy beaches of Malibu, skied the Rocky Mountains, and tasted wine in half the wineries in Sonoma County and Napa Valley. They went to Mardi Gras, the Super Bowl, and watched the ball drop in Times Square on New Year's Eve. Then, on a rainy morning in late April, Lia woke up in a seedy motel in Las Vegas with the worst hangover of her life. She'd lost a small fortune at the casinos, and she knew it was time to cut back on the boozing. It took her less than twenty-four hours to realize that Justin wasn't nearly as much fun sober. Their chemistry had fizzled along with her money.

Lia peeled off from the group and ducked into her bed-and-breakfast. She climbed the stairs to her corner room on the front of the old Victorian house. Opening her suitcase on the bed, she dumped her clothes inside. In the bathroom, she raked her toiletries into her cosmetic bag. A plastic pill bottle missed the bag and bounced off the floor. She picked up the bottle and shook it. Only one pill left. The doctors had prescribed lithium when they diagnosed her with bipolar disorder two years ago. She rubbed the scars on her wrists. It had taken a suicide attempt for them to figure out what Lia had suspected for years.

She hated taking the medicine. She no longer wanted to feel like a zombie. Justin had taught her how to live again. She loved feeling the sun on her face and the wind in her hair and her heart beating in her chest as she jogged down the beach. She dumped the pill in the toilet. To avoid leaving behind evidence of her identity, she dropped the empty bottle into her bag.

Placing her cosmetic bag in her suitcase, she zipped it up, then wheeled it down the stairs and out the side door of the bed-and-breakfast. She hailed a taxi to the bus station and bought a ticket on the next bus heading out of Key West. From Orlando, she would venture east to the ocean and find a small beach town where she could lay low until things with Ricky's murder investigation settled down. If she ate little and stayed in a modest hotel, she would have enough money to last two weeks. From there, when the timing was right, she'd return to Charleston and work a deal with her sister. She had no room in her life for snotty noses and bedtime stories. She would give up her twins in exchange for her freedom. She believed with her whole rotten heart that Bella and Mya would be better off without her for a mother. But the price tag would be high. And her sister had the money to afford them.

ELLIE

*E*llie presented her business card to the desk sergeant. "I'd like to speak to Detective Hamlin about the Ricky Bertram case."

The sergeant peered at her over his reading glasses. "And what, exactly, is your relationship to the case?"

"I'm Ricky's sister-in-law. I'm here from Charleston, looking for my sister."

The sergeant summoned his coworker from the other end of the desk. "Drake, take these people to the back. And let Detective Hamlin know they're here."

They followed Officer Drake down a long, narrow hallway and into an interview room. The room was bare—aside from the one-way mirror, a wooden table, and four chairs that were positioned in the center of the tiny room.

Ellie waited for Officer Drake to leave before going to stand in front of the one-way mirror. "Do you think they're watching us right now?" she said, smoothing her frizzy hair into a ponytail.

"Probably. Why don't we get naked and give them a show?" Julian said, wiggling his eyebrows at her.

"Ha ha. That would be funny . . . if the situation wasn't so serious," she said as she sat down in the empty chair beside him.

Detective Hamlin entered the room and shook hands with Ellie and then Julian. With his deep tan and mop of golden curls, he looked the part of a Floridian homicide detective. He took a seat across from them and rifled through a stack of papers. "Here it is." He slipped on a pair of wire reading glasses. "I received a report from the Charleston PD. I appreciate your cooperation in answering their questions." His blue eyes skimmed the report. "It says here that you and your sister aren't close. If that's the case, what motivated you to fly all the way down here from Charleston?"

It irritated her that he hadn't bothered to read the report. "That's correct, Detective. Lia and I were separated when we were very young. If you'd done your homework, you'd know this," she said in an accusatory tone. "Like I told the officers yesterday, our past history is not pertinent to your case. My sister was having some problems in her marriage. I assume you know about Ricky's gambling debts."

The detective nodded. "We're aware of his financial difficulties."

"I gave Lia some money from the inheritance I'd received from our grandmother to start a new life for herself and the girls. But she disappeared instead, leaving the girls in my care. I haven't heard from her in seven months. When the officers in Charleston told me a woman matching Lia's description was wanted for questioning in the murder of her husband, I came down here hoping to find my sister. I need to make some decisions regarding the girls' future. But I can't do that without help from their biological mother."

Hamlin's face softened and his lips curled into a smile that revealed pearly white teeth. "I can understand that. I'm sorry she's making things difficult for you."

Ellie retrieved the folded photograph of the mystery woman

from her tote and placed it on the table in front of him. "I understand from the manager at the hotel that this woman is your prime suspect. But this is not my sister."

Hamlin squinted at the picture. "Are you sure? The photograph is grainy. If you and your sister aren't close, do you even know her well enough to make the identity?"

Ellie was grateful for Julian's quiet presence beside her. "Lia has a medium-size, oval-shaped burn scar on her neck. She usually wears turtlenecks to cover up the scar. At least she did during our brief time together last fall. I can't imagine she'd be wearing them in this climate. Regardless, I've spoken with the hotel manager. This woman wears revealing clothing and has no such scar."

Julian tapped his finger on the photograph. "We just spotted this woman on Duval Street while eating lunch at DJ's Clam Shack. I approached her casually. When I asked if she knew the Bertrams, she took off. I tried to catch her, but I lost her in the crowd."

Hamlin's body went still. "When did you say this happened?"

Julian glanced at his watch. "About thirty minutes ago. We came straight here."

"Let me see if I can get some men on it. Excuse me a minute." Detective Hamlin left the room. By the time he returned—forty-five minutes later—Ellie was livid at him for keeping them waiting.

"I'm sorry, folks. I was in with Joey Bertram, Ricky's brother. He's just come from identifying his brother's body at the morgue."

"May I speak with him?" Ellie asked. "He may know something about Lia's whereabouts."

"Technically, I can't arrange a meeting for you. But he's in the hallway now. I can't stop you from speaking to him on your way out."

"Thank you, Detective." Ellie returned the mystery woman's photograph to her bag and stood up.

The detective held the door open for them while they exited the room. There was only one other person in the hallway—a man with a shaved head. Joey Bertram, his face pinched in anger, was leaning against the wall with his arms crossed over his muscular chest. When Ellie introduced herself, he ignored her offer of a handshake.

"Since when did Lia have a sister?" he snarled.

Ellie retracted her hand and held her shoulders high, refusing to be bullied. "Since seven months ago. It's a long story. We were separated when we were young. I'm looking for Lia. Do you have any idea where she might be? She left Bella and Mya in my care."

He stared at her with a blank expression.

"You don't know who Bella and Mya are, do you?" She didn't wait for him to respond. "They're your nieces, Ricky's three-year-old twin daughters. When's the last time you spoke with your brother, Mr. Bertram?"

He shrugged. "Five years ago, when he told me he was leaving Wendy, a perfectly wonderful woman and wife, to marry your sister. Your sister's a money whore. She was always pressuring him to buy things they couldn't afford. No wonder he ended up in financial trouble."

Ellie suddenly felt light-headed and leaned into her husband for support.

Resting his hand on the small of her back, Julian asked, "And how would you know any of this if you haven't spoken to your brother in five years?"

"From friends and family. Everyone except Ricky knows Lia's a good-for-nothing slut."

Detective Hamlin stepped in between them. "Let's dispense with the name calling, Mr. Bertram. Mrs. Hagood is searching for her sister regarding a family matter."

"I don't give a rip about her family matter," Joey said, pushing himself off the wall. "Her sister drove a knife into my brother's chest just as sure as I'm standing here."

Heat flushed through Ellie's body and beads of perspiration broke out on her forehead. "For your information, Mr. Bertram, the woman staying with Ricky at the Buena Vista is not my sister." She snapped the photograph open in front of his face. "Either this mystery woman killed him, or the men he owed a lot of money finally caught up with him."

"Ricky was too smart to get caught by any loan shark." He studied the picture closely. "Whoever that is didn't mean nothing to Ricky. He always had women falling all over him. Which is why I'm surprised he fell for a tramp like Lia." Joey looked past Ellie at the detective. "Find this woman's sister, Detective Hamlin, and you've got yourself the killer."

Ellie planted her fists on her hips. "Since you know so much, Mr. Bertram, what motivation would my sister have for murdering your brother?"

He coughed into his hand. "His million-dollar life insurance policy for starters."

Ellie worked hard not to let her surprise show. "And you know about this life insurance how?"

"Because I'm the one who sold it to him." He removed his wallet from his back pocket and fished out a business card. "It just so happens, I'm in the insurance business. I advised my brother against it, but he insisted on naming Lia as the beneficiary."

She stared at the card in his hand, but she didn't take it from him. "You're wrong. Lia didn't need money. She and I recently inherited a very large estate from our grandmother."

Ugh! I don't like stretching the truth, but this man's arrogance is infuriating.

When she turned abruptly away from him, a sudden wave of dizziness caused her to stumble. Hamlin and Julian grabbed hold of her and helped her to a nearby bench.

Julian knelt beside her. "Are you okay, honey? Do you feel like you're going to faint?"

Ellie rested her head against the back of the bench. "I'm okay. I just felt lightheaded." She noticed the detective's concerned expression. "I'm pregnant, Detective."

"That explains a lot." He held up a finger. "Wait here. I know just what you need." He hurried down the hall and disappeared into a room on the left. He was back in a flash with a small plastic bottle of apple juice. "I have three children, Mrs. Hagood. My wife had trouble with low blood sugar during all of her pregnancies."

Ellie unscrewed the lid and gulped down the apple juice. She glared at Joey Bertram, who was hovering near them.

"Give the lady some privacy, please," Hamlin said. "Why don't you wait for me in my office? Last door on the left at the end of the hall."

"I'm sorry if I upset you, Mrs. Hagood." Joey tipped his hat to Ellie and retreated down the hall.

"Feeling any better?" Julian asked.

Ellie nodded. "Much."

"I'm sorry he was so rude to you," Hamlin said. "I'd better go deal with him before he insults my staff. Thank you for coming in today, Mrs. Hagood. If anything else occurs to you that might help in our investigation, I would appreciate hearing from you." He handed her a business card. "Please feel free to call me anytime."

"Likewise." Ellie scribbled Julian's cell number on the back of one of her business cards. "I'm not sure of our plans yet, but we'll probably stay in town through the weekend. We're at the Buena Vista. You have all of our numbers. Please let me know if you locate my sister. I desperately need to speak with her about the children."

"I understand. Like I said, I'm a father myself. I'll do everything I can to help you."

*E*llie and Julian spent the rest of the day combing the downtown area for signs of Lia. They flashed her photograph to the waitstaff at restaurants and desk clerks at any establishment offering overnight accommodations to tourists. But not one person, much to Ellie's dismay, recognized her sister. Exhausted and downhearted, they returned to their hotel, stretched out on the bed, and fell into a deep sleep.

The concierge at the Buena Vista recommended Michaels for dinner. Feeling refreshed after their nap, they opted to walk the mile to the restaurant to take advantage of the sweet tropical breeze. They shared the grilled-scallop salad as their starter. Then Ellie ordered the mahi-mahi, and Julian the pepper-encrusted tuna for their main courses.

"We might as well go home tomorrow," Ellie said over the decadent chocolate volcano for dessert. "I miss the girls, and this search is pointless. Lia is not in Key West."

Julian forked off a bite of his key lime pie. "I say we stay until Sunday. As Abbott reminded us, we never took a honeymoon, and once the baby comes, it'll be difficult to get away. Why not indulge ourselves for one day?"

"But the girls—"

"Are fine with your father. Seriously, Ellie, they love Abbott, and he adores them. Let them have this time together." He reached for her hand. "I'll make love to you all night long if you'll stay."

Ellie admitted the idea sounded appealing. "How can I possibly say no to romance?"

"Who said anything about romance? I'm talking about crazy, uninhibited sex."

Ellie's face grew warm. "Stop! You're making me bashful. Let's change the subject. I can't believe the twins are turning four in a couple of weeks. I'd love to throw a party for them, but I'm fresh out of experience when it comes to children's birthdays."

"Hmm. Let me think." Julian crossed his arms as he sipped his decaf coffee. "I have some friends who live nearby with children about their age. Why don't we plan a Sunday afternoon cookout for children and parents? That way the girls can make a few friends in the neighborhood, and you can meet some of the moms."

"That's a great idea," Ellie said. "Sunday seems like the ideal time to have a party like that. Do you think we can get it all together by then?"

"Sure! Leave everything to me. We'll keep it low-key, with a handful of families and burgers on the grill."

"Maybe Katie can come," Ellie suggested. "The twins would love that."

The enthusiasm disappeared from his face. "I've got her next weekend, not the following."

"Doesn't hurt to ask. She's missed so many weekends this spring, maybe Laura will let her come both. Her soccer season should be over by then."

"That's true. This weekend is her last tournament." Julian tilted his head to the side as he considered the idea. "I'll mention it to Katie and see what she says."

They discussed the birthday party at length as they strolled back to the hotel. For Julian's sake, she tried not to think about Lia, but she found herself searching the faces on the street for her sister.

"You need to relax, honey," Julian said during the elevator ride up to their floor. "All this stress isn't good for the baby. Why don't we go for a moonlight swim?"

Ellie reluctantly agreed, and the warm water relaxed her muscles and calmed her nerves. As promised, Julian delivered an unforgettable night of passion.

EARLY THE NEXT MORNING, when thoughts of Lia plagued her sleep, Ellie left Julian in bed and went out for a walk. After three hours of pounding the pavement in search of her sister, she gave up and returned to the hotel. She ordered hot tea from the outdoor café and called her father to report in.

"No luck, Dad. I don't think she's in Key West." She explained about the mystery woman, their encounter with Joey Bertram, and his reference to his brother's million-dollar life insurance policy. "We might as well come home this afternoon."

"Oh no, you don't! You're not cutting in on my time with Bella and Mya. We have a big day planned. After we photograph the Angel Tree, I promised I'd take them to the aquarium and then to Fleet Landing for dinner. The weather is perfect for eating outside on the deck."

The enthusiasm in her father's voice brought a smile to Ellie's face. "In that case, we'll stay another night. But only if you're sure."

"I'm absolutely positive. You and Julian enjoy yourselves. We'll see you when we see you." Abbott hung up before Ellie could object.

She ordered a coffee for Julian and went up to the room. He

was in the bathroom shaving when she arrived. "What should we do today?" she asked, wrapping her arms around him from behind and resting her head against his back.

He wiped the remnants of shaving cream from his face and turned around to face her. He kissed her lightly on the lips. "We'll decide after I ravish your sexy body." He scooped her off her feet and carried her to the bed.

They spent an hour in bed and another thirty minutes in the shower together. After devouring lobster BLTs for lunch at the Six-Toed Cat, they joined the long line of tourists waiting to tour Ernest Hemingway's home. Next, they visited the Audubon House and the Truman Little White House. They even had their picture taken in front of the marker at the Southernmost Point. By the time they got back to the hotel, around three o'clock, they were ready to relax by the pool. Ellie was lying on her belly, reading Elin Hilderbrand's summer release, when a shadow appeared on the ground beside her. Shielding her eyes against the sun, she was surprised to find Detective Hamlin looming over her.

"Detective, what're you doing here?" she said, scrambling into a sitting position.

"I'm actually here on police business, but I'm glad I saw you. It saves me a phone call. The woman staying with Ricky Bertram at the Buena Vista has been identified as Carrie Doyle. Since the night of the murder, she's been staying at Hawks Cay Resort up at Duck Key."

Ellie's face lit up. "That's good news! Did she confess to the murder?"

"I wish it were that simple." He dragged a chair over from a nearby table and sat down. "I've been questioning her for most of the afternoon. She claims she was at the bar in the lobby here, at the hotel, during the time of the murder. Which is why I'm here. I've just spoken to the bartender, who remembers seeing her.

She's quite a looker. The slinky dress she was wearing that night made an unforgettable impression on him."

"I failed to ask you something yesterday," she said. "At the time, it seemed immaterial. At least to me. But did the medical examiner determine a time of death?"

"Yes. Ricky was wearing a watch that night. An expensive Cartier that Miss Doyle claims she bought for him. The watch was broken in the struggle. The ME's other calculations support that eight fifty was the time of death."

"And this bartender is certain Miss Doyle was at the bar during this time?"

He nodded. "She asked for the check at nine o'clock. He has the receipt to prove it. After she left the bar, Miss Doyle went outside to smoke a cigarette. She claims she saw your sister hurrying out of the side entrance of the hotel. My partner is studying the surveillance video now."

Ellie watched a group of rowdy children playing in the pool while she considered the implications. "How does she know it was Lia? Did she ever meet her?"

"She said she'd never met her but had seen pictures. We lifted a fingerprint from the light switch at the crime scene. It matches your sister's. She's in our database from a misdemeanor arrest several years ago." Hamlin drew in a deep breath and let it out slowly. "There's more. Carrie Doyle was pressuring Ricky to divorce his wife so he could marry her. When Ricky refused to consider it, she took matters into her own hands. She bought a cheap cell phone and texted Lia from it. Pretending to be Ricky, she suggested Lia come to Key West to discuss their future. She arranged a meeting between them at nine o'clock on the night of the murder. She confessed the truth to Ricky that afternoon and persuaded him to meet with Lia. Not only is she seductive, Carrie Doyle is a very wealthy woman. I can see how Ricky would have a difficult time saying no to her."

"Does she still have this cell phone?" Ellie asked.

He removed a plastic bag with a flip phone in it from his pocket as evidence. "The texts corroborate her story." He put the phone back in his pocket. "Miss Doyle was at the lobby bar for a reason. She was watching the front door, waiting for Lia to show up for the meeting."

"And after Lia arrived, Miss Doyle asked for the check and went outside to smoke her cigarette," Ellie said. "If all this is true, why did she run? Why not go to the police?"

"She claims she freaked out and wasn't thinking straight."

Ellie chewed on the arm of her sunglasses. "Whether she killed Ricky or merely stumbled upon his dead body, Lia is probably long gone by now as well."

"Look." Hamlin planted his elbows on his knees. "I'll be honest with you. There are holes in her story that we're checking out. But my hunch is she's not the one who killed Ricky. She loved him too much."

Ellie wrapped her towel around her shoulders and swung her legs over the side of the lounge chair. "So you've crossed this Doyle woman off your list of suspects, which leaves the loan shark and my sister."

"That's not entirely accurate. All three of the above remain on my persons-of-interest list." Hamlin got up and returned his chair to the table. "I'm sorry, Mrs. Hagood. I wish I had better news for you."

"My husband and I are headed back to Charleston tomorrow, Detective. You have my number. Please let me know what, if anything, you find out about Lia."

Hamlin promised he would and left her sitting there alone, her lounge chair an island of despair among a sea of euphoric vacationers. She'd so hoped to leave Key West with her sister's signature on the adoption papers. Lia could be anywhere. If she hadn't spent all the money Ellie had given her, she could be halfway around the world already. In Hawaii or Europe. She wasn't dead. That much Ellie knew.

At least she wasn't dead three nights ago when Carrie Doyle spotted her right here in this very hotel. We'll never find her now. Julian was right. We'll have to proceed with the legal guardianship and then the adoption without my sister's approval.

Lia had left them no choice.

Ellie did her best to put on a pleasant face during dinner at Seven Fish that night, but all she could think about was getting home to the girls. She vowed to stop obsessing over her sister's whereabouts and start focusing on the positive things in her life. The workmen would soon finish her kitchen, and she would share news about her pregnancy with her father. She had a gallery opening and the twins' birthday party to plan. She had her art students to think about and her own work to concentrate on.

They turned in before ten that night in anticipation of an early departure for the airport the following day. Exhausted from the events of the previous days, Ellie fell sound asleep. The loud ringing of her cell phone woke her during the night. She sat bolt upright and groped for her phone on the bedside table. She didn't recognize the number. When she accepted the call, she heard faint breathing on the other end.

"Hello! Is anyone there?" She heard a click, and the line went dead.

Propped on one elbow, rubbing the sleep from his eyes, Julian asked, "Who was that?"

"I have no idea. Whoever it was hung up. It's a Charleston area code. I don't recognize the number, do you?" she asked, holding her phone out for him to see.

He glanced down at the number. "Not off the top of my head."

"I hope nothing happened to Dad or the girls." She was staring at the phone, deciding whether to try back, when it rang again. This time she was greeted by muffled crying that sounded like a child's.

"Mya? Bella? Is that you? What's wrong, sweetheart?"

Again, the line went dead. This time, Ellie quickly returned the call. It rang four times and went into voice mail. A raspy woman's voice announced that the Fuquas were unavailable to answer the phone, but to please leave a message at the beep.

"Fuqua," she said out loud. It took her a minute to place the name. "Oh my god! Ruby's in trouble."

Julian shook his head to clear it. "Who's Ruby?"

"One of my students. I'm sure you've heard me talk about her. She's the one with so much talent." She redialed the number again and again, but each time it went into voice mail. She fell back against the pillows. "The last time I saw Ruby was during class on Thursday. I placed my hand on her shoulder while we were discussing her project. She winced, and I saw bruises on her neck. I pulled her aside after class and asked if she was having trouble at home. She assured me everything was fine, but I gave her my business card anyway and told her to call me anytime. Should I contact the police?"

"I don't know, honey. I can't make that decision for you. If she's in danger, dragging the police into it could make it worse."

"Or it could save her life."

ELLIE

*E*llie never closed her eyes again that night. She was showered, dressed, and packed by the time the sun came up. She waited thirty minutes before calling the principal at Peninsula Elementary. Rose Bellamy was less than thrilled at being disturbed so early on a Sunday morning. She grumbled something about looking into the situation and warned Ellie about getting personally involved with her students.

She tossed the phone on the bed beside Julian. "Am I supposed to just ignore it when there's a chance a child is in danger?"

"I don't know, honey. That's a sensitive situation." He rolled out of bed and staggered half-asleep to the bathroom.

Julian rarely got upset with her, but the combination of his silence and sullen expression from that moment through checkout at the hotel and the drive to the airport spoke for itself —he was irritated. She waited until they were buckled into their first-class seats, the only ones available for their return trip home, to speak.

"I'm sorry, Julian, for dragging you down here on this wild-goose chase and for keeping you awake all night, tossing and turning. I don't blame you for being annoyed with me."

He thumbed her cheek. "I'm not annoyed, Ellie. I'm worried about you. I don't need to remind you that your pregnancy is high risk. All this stress isn't good for you or the baby."

Tears welled up in her eyes. She wanted this baby so much. If something happened to it because of anything she'd done, she'd never forgive herself. "You're right. We've waited long enough for Lia to sort out her life. We need to schedule an appointment with Tyler to discuss how to proceed with the adoption."

"I'll get in touch with him first thing in the morning." He brought her hand to his lips. "I promise everything's going to work out the way it's meant to."

Ellie wished she felt as optimistic as Julian. A gnawing doubt in her gut warned her that things would get a lot worse before they got better.

ELLIE FELT the urge to paint. Her fingers longed to hold the brush, but her canvas remained blank when she stood in front of it in her studio later that afternoon. When Julian took the kids and the dogs to the park across the street, she gave up on getting any work done and went with him. While the girls chased the dogs, Julian and Ellie stretched out on a blanket and discussed plans for the twins' birthday party.

"Dad looked tired when he left," Ellie said, rolling over flat on her back.

Julian snickered. "I think the girls wore him out."

"I'm sure they did, but he'll never admit it."

"Why didn't you break the news about the baby?"

Ellie picked a twig off the blanket and broke it in half. "I'm too tired today. I want to enjoy the moment. I thought we'd tell him when he comes for dinner on Wednesday night. We can celebrate the baby while we christen the kitchen."

"Oh boy!" Julian clapped his hands. "We'll make it a party. What should I cook? Mexican? Italian? Thai?" His eyes got big. "I know. What about a turkey dinner with all the traditional Thanksgiving fixings?"

She mussed his wiry hair. With all his new appliances and gadgets, he was as giddy with delight as a boy in a sporting goods store. "Whatever you decide is fine with me—as long as it's not pizza."

ELLIE WAS grateful when Monday morning arrived. The structure of the work week made her feel more like herself. After a brisk forty-five-minute walk along the seawall and through the neighboring streets, she returned home to find the girls eating Pop-Tarts at the small table in her studio with Maddie.

Maddie hauled herself out of her chair when she saw Ellie watching them from the doorway. "How'd your trip go, Miss Ellie? Did you have any luck finding your"—she cast a glance at the twins—"your friend?"

"Unfortunately, no. Have you seen Julian this morning?"

"Yes'm. He's poking around in the kitchen with the workmen. You ready for your coffee?" Without waiting for Ellie to answer, Maddie went to the Keurig machine she'd set up on a card table in the corner of the room and brewed a cup for Ellie. "I'm so excited about that fancy new kitchen, I can hardly stand it. Mr. Julian says it's gonna be ready on Wednesday. I'm cooking you something special for dinner that night."

Ellie laughed. "I'm sorry, Maddie, but Julian's got first dibs on dinner Wednesday night."

"Then I'll bake something for dessert. And I'll make breakfast for you on Thursday morning." Her dark eyes stared up at the ceiling as she considered what to make. "Waffles. No . . . pancakes. No . . . eggs. What should it be, girls?" she asked the twins.

"Waffles!" they cried in unison.

"You heard them, Maddie. Waffles it is." Ellie went to the table and kissed the top of each of their heads. "But no more Pop-Tarts after Wednesday except on special occasions."

Their lips turned down, and frown lines appeared on their foreheads.

"Don't give me those sad faces. The two of you have eaten enough Pop-Tarts during this kitchen renovation to last for the rest of your lives." Ellie crumbled up the empty Pop-Tart foil wrapping. "Becca will be here soon. Run along upstairs to your room and get dressed. I already laid your clothes out for you."

As they watched the girls skip down the hall hand in hand, Maddie lowered her voice and said, "I'm telling you what, Miss Ellie. My heart done jumped right out of my chest when I heard about Miss Lia's husband. Do you think she done murdered him?"

"I honestly don't know, Maddie." Ellie sank down to a chair at the table. "She's unstable, but I can't imagine her killing her husband with a butcher knife. I never met Ricky Bertram, but he's the girls' father. Whether he was a good guy or not, it makes me sad to think they will grow up without a father. Like Lia and I did, without our mother."

"Them girls have loving parents in you and Mr. Julian. Giving birth to chil'run doesn't make a woman a good mother. God has brought them girls to you for a reason. He's counting on you and Mr. Julian to do right by them."

Tears blurred her vision as she stared up at Maddie. "Do you really believe that, Maddie?"

Maddie placed her hand over her ample chest. "With all my heart."

Ellie swiped at her eyes with the back of her hand. "You don't know how much I needed to hear that."

ELLIE SHOWERED, dressed, and sequestered herself in her studio for the rest of the morning. She felt guilty for not going to her gallery to check on the workmen's progress, but she knew the sounds of construction would only exacerbate her dull headache until it became a full-fledged migraine. Home was quiet for a change with just the swish of the painters' brushes as they finished touching up the trim in the kitchen.

At least my commercial painters are accomplishing something. But not me.

Without once lifting her brush, she stared for hours at her two current works in progress, both oils—one of a storm rolling in over the Charleston harbor, and the other a pair of humming-birds inspired by one of her father's photographs. She finally gave up and took her sketchpad and graphite pencils out to the terrace. She reclined on the chaise lounge with eyes closed as she considered the detail of the image foremost in her mind. Her pencil flew across the paper as she portrayed the child—cheeks and nose speckled with freckles, eyes sparkling with life through thick lashes, wisps of frizzy hair framing her face. When she was finished, she held the sketchpad at a distance and admired her drawing of Ruby.

She'd hoped to hear back from Rose Bellamy, and was disappointed that she hadn't. She promised Julian she would stop obsessing about her young student, but she couldn't help herself. She sensed something was desperately wrong in the child's life. She'd given Ruby her business card with the understanding that she would be there for her if she needed her. The child had tried to get in touch with her twice, in the middle of the night, which was a cry for help if ever there was one.

Tucking her sketchbook under her arm, she went to her computer in her studio and searched the online white pages for the Fuqua family. She came up with a list of ten names in and around the Charleston area, but only one was in the Peninsula Elementary School district. Seeing no harm in driving by the house, she jotted the address onto a sticky note.

She left her desk and went out into the hall. The house was silent. There were no saws or hammers, no music blaring from the painters' portable radio. When she saw that the door to Julian's study was closed, she decided not to disturb him. She wouldn't be gone long enough for him to miss her. She considered riding her bike, but decided against it. The Fuqua address was only a mile or so away, but she was unsure about the safety of the neighborhood. She retrieved her keys from the console table and was on her way out the back door when her decorator arrived.

"I left you a message," Jackie said, looking fashionable as ever in a black-and-white color-block dress. "I hope this a convenient time for us to deliver your breakfast table and chairs."

Ellie checked her phone. "I didn't get your message. Are you sure you dialed the right number?"

"Sorry. I probably dialed your house number by mistake. My delivery guys are on the way. I can wait for them if you need to leave." Jackie removed her Gucci sunglasses and peered over Ellie's shoulder into the kitchen. "This place is really taking shape." She brushed past her and entered the kitchen. She circled the island before moving to the bank of windows on the north side of the room. "I think you'll be pleased when you see the finished product. Reclaimed oak was the ideal choice for the table, and the upholstered cushion for the bench seat turned out just as I'd hoped."

"I've been pleased with everything you've done for me so far, Jackie. I'm sure I'll love the table as well. Unfortunately, I have to run out on an errand. Can you handle the delivery?"

A look of disappointment crossed Jackie's face. "I was hoping to see your reaction, but I understand."

"I promise I'll call you as soon as I get back. Make yourself at home. Maddie is in the house somewhere if you need anything." Ellie exited the house before Jackie could object.

Using Google Maps for guidance, she navigated her Mini Cooper through the downtown streets, each appearing progressively more run-down as she approached her destination. Huckleberry Court sounded like a pleasant place to live, but the ramshackle houses lining the street suggested otherwise. The Fuquas' home, a "single house"—named as such because of its single-room width—was no different. The yard was mostly dirt, aside from a few tufts of weeds. The side porch, slanted with rotten newel posts, housed the family's collection of junk—a rusted-out refrigerator, plastic patio furniture, and rolled-up carpet remnants. There were no cars parked on the street, and shades were pulled down over the windows. As she idled in front of the house, Ellie said a silent prayer that Ruby was in school where she belonged. Where she was safe from whatever bad things happened to her in this house at night.

ELLIE

*E*llie arrived at school early on Tuesday, hoping for a chance to speak with the principal before her class started, but Rose Bellamy was in a meeting and could not be disturbed. She held her breath as her students filed into the room, hoping to see Ruby's enthusiastic face and bright eyes. But the last student arrived with no sign of Ruby. She waited until the other students were settled.

"Does anyone know where Ruby is? Is she absent today?" She managed to sound casual despite the panic rising in her chest.

"Don't you get the absentee list, Mrs. Hagood?" Terrell asked. "Ruby hasn't been to school all week."

None of the faculty had ever mentioned an absentee list to Ellie. More evidence the other teachers didn't take her seriously. She was a volunteer, teaching a frivolous art class to a select group of students.

Nikki sent an elbow to Terrell's ribs. "It's only Tuesday, dummy. She's probably just sick."

"I'm sure that's it," Ellie said, but she suspected Ruby's absence was related to more than the common cold.

Her students' excitement over finishing their self-portraits boosted her spirits, but after class, she marched down to the office and demanded to see the principal. The secretary's efforts to ward off Ellie failed when she noticed Rose Bellamy's door cracked and barged right in.

"Did you find out anything about Ruby Fuqua?" she asked as she approached the desk. "She was absent yesterday and today. I'm extremely worried about her, Rose."

"I contacted a friend who works for the South Carolina Department of Social Services," Rose said, her eyes remaining on the computer. "I haven't heard back from her yet. I'll be sure to let you know when I do."

Ellie knew the middle-aged black woman more through reputation than experience. She'd had minimum interaction with the principal since she'd started volunteering at the school. From what she'd heard, Rose kept her students in line with strict disciplinary tactics. Ellie was not an expert, but in her mind, elementary students required equal amounts of nurturing and discipline.

"I mean no disrespect, Rose, but that's not good enough. This child's life might be in danger."

Rose turned away from the computer and stood to face Ellie. "Do you have any proof that Ruby is the one who called you on Saturday night?"

Ellie held her phone out to the principal. "I still have the number. The police can easily trace it."

Rose glanced down at the phone and flinched. "Hold on a minute. It is way too premature to get the police involved. What prompted you to give Ruby your number in the first place?"

Ellie took a deep breath, thinking, *I will not let this self-important woman intimidate me.*

"I explained all that to you when we spoke on the phone Sunday morning. In class last week, I placed a hand on Ruby's shoulder as we were discussing her self-portrait project, and she winced as though in pain."

"But did you actually see any bruises?"

"Yes, as a matter of fact, I did."

"Did you ever consider that maybe the child fell off her bicycle?" Rose asked.

That was the explanation Ruby had provided, but Ellie doubted the child owned a bicycle. "Ruby hasn't been her usual bright self for the past few weeks. I have a feeling something is very wrong in her life."

"You've done all you can do for now," Rose said, returning her attention to her computer. "Please close the door on your way out."

Ellie stared down at the top of the principal's head, noticing the bald spots where her hair was thinning. "I'm required by law to report it if I suspect a child may be being abused at home. If it happens again, I will call the police."

Rose's head shot up. "You do what you think best." She pointed her slim, manicured finger at Ellie. "But I'll remind you, you are not employed by this school. You are strictly here on a volunteer basis—a situation that can be terminated at any point."

Anger surged through Ellie's body. "And I'll remind *you* that I'm donating my time to enrich the lives of children who would not otherwise have an opportunity to explore the world of art."

"You're not indispensable, Mrs. Hagood. Anyone on my staff can teach these students how to color pictures."

Bracing herself against the desk, Ellie leaned in close to Rose. "Whether I'm a paid employee or not, you have no right to speak to me like this."

The principal jabbed her finger toward the door. "You may leave now. And don't bother coming back. Your services at this school are no longer needed."

Ellie straightened. "Fine. I'll leave. But you haven't seen the last of me. I plan to report this incident, including your insolent attitude toward me and complete disregard for a child's well-being, to the school board."

ELLIE RACED her Mini across town for the meeting Julian had arranged with their attorney to discuss adoption proceedings for the twins. She arrived fifteen minutes late.

"I'm so sorry," Ellie said when Tyler and Julian stood to greet her. "I got tied up at the elementary school."

"No worries," Tyler said.

Ellie approved of the young attorney, who had represented Julian in his divorce from his first wife and custody battle over Katie. Despite his age, Tyler's extensive knowledge of the law instilled confidence in them. She wanted him on her side in the courtroom. She sensed a controlled aggression simmering beneath his cool outward composure.

"Your husband was just bringing me up to speed on the events of the past week." Tyler said, motioning her to sit on the sofa next to Julian.

As she took her seat, she gave Julian's arm a squeeze, an apology for being late. He smiled and winked at her in return. She crossed her legs and clasped her hands together in her lap to stop them from shaking. She was a wreck after her confrontation with Rose and then rushing to get to the meeting on time. Facing a wall of windows in Tyler's office that overlooked the harbor, she stared out across the glistening water at Fort Sumter and forced Rose and Ruby from her mind.

"So you know my sister is at the top of the list of suspects in her husband's murder," Ellie said. "How do these new developments affect our case? I don't mean to sound crass, but we no longer have to worry about the legal rights of the father since he's no longer alive. Lia being wanted for murder, though, doesn't speak well for her character."

Tyler steepled his fingers. "That may be so, but she is still their mother. All reasonable efforts to locate the biological parents must be made. Your recent trip to Key West will help your case in that regard. However, by South Carolina law, child abandonment occurs when a parent willfully deserts a child or surrenders physical possession of a child without making adequate arrangements for the child's needs. In your sister's case, she made adequate arrangements for the girls' needs by leaving them in your care. Based on what you've told me in previous meetings, you offered to keep the girls while your sister figured out her life. She understood you had the means to provide for them. On the flip side is the lack of meaningful communication with the child or caregiver for a period of three months."

Julian glanced at Ellie and then back at Tyler. "What exactly are you saying?"

"I'm saying that you are facing a long, complicated process. This letter"—he opened a file on his lap and held up a photographed copy of Lia's letter—"grants you temporary custody. No court will argue that. But to permanently adopt the girls, the South Carolina Department of Social Services will require an investigation to determine that you are mentally and financially capable of taking care of your nieces."

"How much time will all that take?" Ellie asked.

"Several months at least."

She gripped the arms of her chair. "I gave my sister the opportunity to straighten out her life, and she took advantage of me. From now on, my nieces are my primary concern. If Lia shows up tomorrow wanting them back, I'll take her to court and fight for them. Any woman who goes seven months without so much as a phone call to her three-year-old daughters doesn't deserve to be their mother."

ELLIE AND JULIAN didn't speak to one another as they rode to the lobby in the elevator. There was no point in starting a conversation they couldn't finish. They would wait until after the twins went to bed that night to discuss what they'd learned at the meeting.

"I'm going to take a drive. I need to be by myself for a while, but I won't be long." She checked the time on her phone. It was nearly five o'clock. "Do you want me to text Becca, to see if she can stay with the twins until I get home?"

"That's not necessary. I'm going home now. I'll take the girls to pick up some dinner. Anything special you're craving?"

She wrapped her arms around his neck. "I'm craving a home-cooked meal."

"Starting tomorrow night, you'll have all the home-cooked meals your heart desires." He kissed her cheek. "I'll surprise you with dinner," he said over his shoulder as they parted on the street.

"Anything but pizza," she called after him.

Ellie seldom let her emotions get the best of her, but on the rare occasion she couldn't hold back any longer, she sought refuge in her car. She maneuvered her Mini out of the parallel parking space and headed off in the opposite direction of home. Tears blurred her vision, and loud sobs filled the empty space in her Mini as she drove aimlessly around town. She had no particular destination in mind, but she wasn't surprised to find herself parking her car in front of the Fuquas' residence. The shades were still drawn, and no one appeared to be at home.

The baby growing in her belly was sucking up most of her energy. Worrying about the twins and Lia and Ruby was sapping the little that remained. She swiped away her tears. She owed it to the baby, and to Julian, to pull herself together. She put the car in gear. As she was pulling away from the curb, a minivan rounded the corner and pulled up in front of the house across the street. A plump-but-attractive woman about Ellie's age got out of the van and walked up the sidewalk. Pink geraniums spilled from planters flanking the yellow front door. Two rocking chairs occupied the front porch, and an American flag hung from one of the columns. The house appeared more loved and cared for than any other on the street.

Ellie got out of her car and jogged across the street. "Excuse me, ma'am. Can I have a moment of your time?"

The woman walked back down the sidewalk to greet her.

Ellie offered her hand. "I'm Ellie Hagood. I teach art at the elementary school."

"And I'm Marta McGinnis. Pleased to make your acquaintance. What can I do for you?"

"I'm curious about your neighbors across the street. Ruby hasn't been in school the past couple of days, and I'm worried about her."

Marta's face grew serious. "I've been worried myself. Strange things have been happening in that house since Gina—that's Ruby's mother—got herself a new live-in boyfriend."

Ellie suddenly felt chilled despite the warm evening. "What kind of things?"

"Shady-looking characters coming and going at all hours of the night. My guess is they're running drugs out of that house. I've been extra careful to lock my doors."

"Do you know what kind of cars they have?" Ellie asked, turning toward the Fuquas' house. "I've driven by a couple of times today, but it doesn't look like anyone's home."

"Gina doesn't have a car," Marta said. "At least as far as I know. I don't think the boyfriend does either. I haven't seen the same vehicle parked over there more than once or twice."

"Does Ruby have any siblings?"

"Nope. She's an only child. She's a sweet girl, like a daughter to me since I don't have any children of my own. She's always eager to help me bring in the groceries or work in the yard. She planted these geraniums for me."

Ellie smiled. "I noticed them. They're lovely. And Ruby is a sweet girl. But she hasn't been her perky self lately, which is why I'm worried about her."

The woman's hazel eyes narrowed. "I haven't seen much of her either in the past week, now that I think about it. You mentioned that she's been absent from school. I hope nothing happened to her. I dismissed it at the time. Folks on this street are always arguing over something or another. But Gina and her boyfriend had a humdinger of a fight over the weekend. I happened to be sleeping with my windows open that night, because my air conditioner was on the fritz. I heard the screaming and yelling all the way in my bedroom at the back of the house."

Panic gripped Ellie's chest. "When, exactly, over the weekend?"

"Sometime past midnight on Saturday night."

ELLIE

*J*ulian and Ellie had just finished putting the girls to bed when he received a call from his daughter. He went into his study and closed the door. Ellie was in her studio going through her emails when he emerged a short time later.

He plopped down on the sofa in front of her desk. "Katie canceled on me for this weekend."

Ellie looked up from her computer. "Oh no! I thought you said her last soccer tournament was last weekend."

"Soccer *is* over. She canceled for a different reason this time. She's been invited to a friend's birthday party. One of the girls on her team is having a mother-daughter campout on Friday night at a lake near Spartanburg. They are going hiking on Saturday."

She left her desk and went to stand in front of him. "It's not my place to say anything, so feel free to tell me to mind my own business. It's not fair for her to cancel on you at the last minute all the time. You need to do something about this situation."

"It is your place to say something. You're my wife and her stepmother." Julian stretched out on the sofa and pulled Ellie down beside him. "Laura is violating our custody agreement. I'm glad you suggested I keep a journal. It gives me proof of her noncompliance. Problem is, if I put my foot down and force her to miss the party, she'll end up resenting me for it. I worry that the older she gets, as her social life becomes more important to her, she'll have a new excuse every weekend and I'll never see her. My life is here, in Charleston, with you. I can't move to Spartanburg, even if I wanted to."

Ellie craned her neck to see him. "Did you talk to Laura on the phone just now?"

"No," he said. "I asked Katie to put her mom on the phone, but Katie said she wasn't available."

Ellie's eyebrows shot up. "Do you think she left Katie all by herself on a weeknight?"

"I don't know. Maybe. Katie said her mother was in the bathtub, but I got the impression she's hiding something. I've dismissed it the times you've mentioned it before, but I think you might be right. I think Laura may be poisoning Katie's mind against us."

"What did she say to make you think that?"

"I told her I was disappointed she wasn't coming this weekend and asked if she'd consider coming the following weekend, for the twins' birthday. She accused me of not loving her anymore now that I have you and the twins. I tried to reassure her that that wasn't the case, but she started crying and hung up on me."

"I'm so sorry, Julian. I know how hard this is for you, having her so far away."

"I need some quality time with her to reconnect, so I can figure out what's going on with her. If she's content with her life, I'll have to settle for driving to Spartanburg once a month for Sunday brunch. If she's not happy, then I'll take her mother to court."

"You'll have two weeks with Katie this summer," Ellie said. "That should give you an opportunity to reconnect. Have you given any thought to how you want to spend your time together?"

"I thought I'd let her have a week in Charleston to visit with her friends, and then rent a house on one of the local beaches for the second week." He snuggled his feet with hers. "Do you have a choice of beaches?"

"Me?" Ellie's face registered surprise. Thus far, Julian had been vague about his plans for his summer vacation with his daughter. She wasn't sure until that moment if she and the twins were even invited. "Any beach sounds heavenly to me right now."

"We'll be lucky if I find any beach rental at this late date."

"You? The popular Julian Hagood? I'm sure you know someone willing to rent their beach house to you for a week."

"Hmm." He paused for a minute as he thought about it. "You're right. I have some ideas. I'll get to work on it right away." He drew an imaginary line with his fingertip from the top of her forehead down her nose to her lips. "I like it when you smile. I'm glad to see you're in a better mood. You seemed rattled earlier at Tyler's office. Your drive must have cleared your head."

Rolling on her side, she placed her back to him while she told him about her confrontation with the Peninsula School principal. "Can you believe it? Rose actually fired me from my volunteer job."

Julian wrapped his arm around her from behind and drew her close. "Your compassion toward other people is one of the things I love most about you. I can see where it would be difficult for you to resist getting involved in your students' lives."

"Not all my students, Julian. Just Ruby." She rolled off the sofa, crossed the room to the Keurig machine, and brewed herself a cup of chamomile tea. "I feel a special connection to Ruby, and I think she feels the same way about me. She reminds me of myself at that age. She puts on a brave face, but I sense she's scared and lonely deep down inside."

Julian joined her in front of the coffee machine. He placed

his hand on her belly. "You need to think about your own safety and the safety of our unborn child. We don't know what's going on with Ruby's home life, but the last thing you need to do is get involved in a domestic dispute."

Ellie looked away from her husband.

I wonder how he'd react if he knew I risked our unborn baby's life today when I drove by and stopped in front of the Fuquas' house.

Not only did they live in an unsafe neighborhood, Marta had speculated that Ruby's mother and boyfriend were dealing drugs. And where there were drug deals, there were shoot-outs.

"You're right," she said in a soft voice. "I'll let the police handle the situation from now on."

He tilted her chin and kissed her lips. "Come on." He took her by the hand. "Let's go play house in our new kitchen. I've started my grocery list. It'll take me four trips to restock the pantry and refrigerator."

"I can help with that, you know." She increased her stride to keep up with him. "You've got to stop pampering me. I know this pregnancy is high risk, but I'm not bedridden. At least not yet."

While Ellie sipped her tea, Julian opened and closed cabinet doors, deciding where the contents of the mountain of boxes piled high in the living room would go. China and glassware. Pots and pans. Eating and cooking utensils. Serving platters and casserole dishes.

"We have so much stuff. Between your house, my apartment in California, and the few of my grandmother's things I decided to keep—it'll take us all summer to get settled." She sat down on the banquette under the window. "What do you think about the table?"

He ran his hand across the top of the table. "I approve of the lighter finish. It shows off the grain in the wood."

Ellie stared down at the aqua-and-coral-striped fabric on the bench. "How smart was it to laminate this fabric with two messy toddlers in the house and a baby on the way?"

"Jackie does a nice job. I'm glad you like working with her." Julian opened a set of bifold doors, revealing a brand-new washer and dryer. "I don't know about you, but I'll be glad to get rid of the other washer and dryer. They're ancient, circa 1949."

Ellie joined him in front of the washer and dryer. "Moving the utility room to the kitchen was a genius idea. Now our guests won't be staring down the hall into the utility room when they come in the front door."

"Instead, they'll be looking at a powder room." She curled her lip up in distaste, and he patted her back. "Don't worry. We'll put a special hinge on the door so it stays closed when not in use."

Converting the current utility room to a powder room was the final stage of their renovation. "I understand the contractor was waiting until the kitchen was finished to gut the utility room, but I'm definitely not looking forward to more construction. How long will it take?"

"A few weeks max. The workmen have promised to stay out of our way as much as possible." He closed the door on the closet, and they turned to face the kitchen." He drew her in for a half hug. "Are you happy with the outcome?"

"Very much so." She rested her head on his shoulder. "Everything is coming together just as I'd hoped. The room is sophisticated without being sterile. It's bright and cheerful, a warm nest for our little brood."

ELLIE

The technicians showed up bright and early on Wednesday morning to install the Carrara marble countertops. As soon as they finished, the plumbers came to hook up the sinks. The last workmen left at two o'clock that afternoon. The contractor arrived shortly thereafter to inspect their work and announced the project complete. Julian left immediately to stock up on groceries at the Harris Teeter while Maddie and Ellie cleaned the kitchen from top to bottom. Ellie unpacked boxes, loading the cabinets with dishes and glassware, while Maddie baked the promised dessert.

"That looks amazing," Ellie said when Maddie removed the bubbling blueberry cobbler from the oven. "Why don't you stay for dinner? We'd love to have you."

"Thanks, Miss Ellie, but I need to get home to my husband. He'll be looking for his supper. But I'll be back first thing tomorrow morning to cook the biggest breakfast you ever seen —waffles for the twins, and breakfast hash for you and Mr. Julian."

Ellie's mouth watered at the thought of breakfast hash—eggs, hash browns, cheese, and sausage cooked together in an iron skillet. "Yum, Maddie. I haven't had breakfast hash since I was a child."

"You just wait. I have lots of recipes up my sleeve." Maddie retrieved her jacket and purse from the utility room and bid her good night.

Julian and Ellie were in the kitchen with the twins when Ellie's father arrived at six o'clock with a bottle of prosecco to christen the new room. He popped the cork and poured three glasses. They clinked in a toast and he circled the room, sipping his wine as he admired the improvements. "You've really done an extraordinary job. The craftsmanship of the cabinets is spectacular."

"My talented architect gets all the credit." Ellie held her glass up again. "To Julian. And to Julian's new job." She pretended to take a sip, then set her glass down on the counter.

"What new job?" Abbott asked.

She looped her arm through her husband's and leaned against him. "My amazing man has just been awarded the Campbell project."

Abbott's dark eyes grew large. "You mean that monster Italianate three blocks south of here?"

"That's the one." Julian had been wearing the same grin since that morning when he'd received the call from Pete Campbell offering him the job.

"That is something to celebrate. Congratulations, son." Abbott lifted his glass to Julian and then drained its contents. He eyeballed Ellie's untouched glass on the counter. "Don't you like the wine?"

She'd planned to wait until after dinner when the twins went to bed, but the moment felt right to break the news. She looked over at the twins, who sat at the table, completely preoccupied with the coloring books Abbott had brought them.

"It's not the wine." She waved away his concern with the flick of her wrist. "I've been feeling a little nauseous lately."

He studied her face intently. "You do look a little green, now that you mention it. Maybe you're coming down with the stomach flu. How long have you been feeling this way?"

A mischievous smile tugged on her lips. "About ten weeks now."

Abbott's jaw hit the marble countertop. "Are you saying what I think you're saying?"

"We have something else to celebrate tonight besides the kitchen and Julian's new project. I'm expecting a baby at the end of September. I'm sorry I didn't tell you sooner. I wanted to wait until I passed the three-month mark." She slid her full wineglass toward him. "I hate to waste this. You might as well enjoy it for me."

"That's amazing news, sweetheart." He lifted her off the ground in a bear hug and then quickly set her down again. "I'm so sorry. I hope I didn't hurt you."

"Please don't fuss. My husband is coddling me enough as it is." Ellie made a silly cross-eyed face at Julian before turning back to her father. "Before you ask, Dad, my pregnancy is considered high risk because of my age, but my doctor has assured me that everything looks good."

He palmed his forehead. "Wow! I haven't felt this excited about anything since . . . well, since I don't know when. Let me have a look at you, sweetheart." He held her at arm's length, examining her from head to toe, his eyes lingering on her belly.

She laughed. "Are you looking for this?" she asked, pulling her tunic taut across her swollen tummy. Her tighter-fitting clothes had gotten snug in the few days since their return from Florida, and she'd begun wearing leggings and loose-fitting tops.

He placed a hand on her belly. "Well, I'll be damned!"

"Shh!" She pressed her finger to her lips. "We haven't told the girls yet."

"I won't say a word." He picked up her full glass of bubbly from the counter and guzzled it down in one gulp.

Julian slapped Abbott on the back. "Take it easy there, buddy. It's too early in the evening to get drunk."

Ellie took the glass away from her father. "We have a long night ahead of us. Julian has planned an elaborate Mexican dinner, and he's selected a different wine for each course. Obviously, not for me. I'll be drinking milk."

"Sorry. I got a little excited." Abbott puffed out his chest. "I'm gonna be a grandpa."

"Remember them?" Julian inclined his head toward the twins. "You're already a GoPa."

"I know. And I love them dearly. But this grandchild is different. This is my Ellie's baby," he said, kissing the top of her head.

A wide smile spread across her face. "That means so much to me, Dad."

Julian set his wineglass down and went to the Sub-Zero integrated refrigerator. He pulled out a bowl of homemade guacamole and placed it, along with a basket of chips, in front of Ellie and Abbott. Then he removed a bowl of lime wedges and several different types of cheeses.

"Good gracious," Abbott said, peering over Julian's shoulder as he crumbled Cotija cheese over a casserole dish. "What exactly is on this elaborate menu of yours?"

"I'm preparing more of a tasting menu, actually. I'm working on vegetarian enchiladas verdes now. I'll also be serving shrimp tostadas and skirt steak fajitas."

"Are Bella and Mya eating all this?" Abbott asked.

"Nah," Julian said, tossing the Cotija package in the trash can. "They're having cheese quesadillas."

Her father chuckled. "I was gonna say—you're a better man than I am if you can get them to eat gourmet food."

Julian slid his casserole in the oven. "It won't be long. Now that the kitchen is finished, I plan to work on them. Under my tutelage, Katie has turned out to be quite the little foodie."

With the volume down low, Ellie tuned their built-in stereo

system to a classic rock station. "So, Dad, what news do you have to report? Have you invited Lacey Sinkler out on a date yet?"

Abbott's face beamed red. "As a matter of fact, yes. I'm taking her to brunch on Saturday at the Hominy Grill."

"Why the Hominy Grill?" Ellie asked. "Don't get me wrong. I love their food, but I thought you'd want to impress her on your first date."

Abbott hunched his shoulders. "I let her make the choice. Besides, she's not the kind of girl I feel the need to impress."

Julian nodded as he sprinkled seasoning on the steak. "That's very true about Lacey. She's a cut-off blue jeans, beer-drinking kinda girl. She's fun and easy to be with."

"I can't wait to meet her. I hope you'll invite her to the twins' birthday party a week from Sunday."

"Let's see how Saturday goes first." Abbott dropped down to the barstool beside him. "Anyway, I have some other news, although mine isn't nearly as exciting as either of yours."

Ellie gave her father a playful shove. "Do tell."

"Beginning in September, I'll be teaching two sections of digital photography at the college." He dragged a chip through the guacamole and stuffed it in his mouth.

"That's awesome, Dad. I know how much you've always wanted to teach." She sat down next to him at the island. "I thought you were planning to travel next fall."

He shrugged. "I've traveled enough to last me a lifetime. I may take a trip every now and then, but I'm ready to establish some roots, especially now with my new grandbaby on the way."

Ellie hung her head. "Maybe you can get a teaching job for me at the college, since I got fired from the elementary school."

Abbott froze, his chip loaded with guacamole suspended in midair. "How does one get fired from a volunteer job?"

"Turns out the administration doesn't like it when their teachers actually care about their students."

While Julian went outside to grill the steak, Ellie told her father about Ruby Fuqua, including her concern that the child was being abused and Ruby's late-night call to Ellie when they were in Florida.

Abbott listened intently, and when she'd finished talking he asked, "Do you think it's a good idea for you to get involved in this situation, considering your condition?"

"Pregnancy isn't a condition, Dad."

"It is when you're high risk."

Her hand shot out. "Say no more. I hear you. Anyway, I met Ruby's neighbor Marta McGinnis yesterday. She seems to really care about Ruby, and promised to keep an eye out for her."

Abbott propped his elbows on the counter and bumped her with his shoulder. "I know how much you care about people, Ellie, and how hard it is for you to ignore a friend in trouble. But you have to think of yourself first for a change."

"I know, Dad. Julian reminds me at least once a day."

"You're not going to have time to teach art anyway, with the twins and the gallery and a baby on the way."

Ellie sighed. "You're probably right, although I was enjoying this particular group of students. They are an eager bunch, and seemed grateful for me being there. Lately I've been regretting my decision to buy the gallery. The studio space above the gallery will give me an opportunity to work away from the house, but I have no interest in greeting customers and no experience in organizing openings."

Julian had returned from outside in the midst of their conversation and was carving the skirt steak into thin strips. "I haven't thought about it until now, but Lacey might be just the person you're looking for to run the gallery," he said as he transferred slices of steak onto a serving platter. "She's responsible and organized, and pays great attention to detail. She's also well immersed in the art scene in Charleston—more an enthusiast than a collector, although she does have a few prized pieces."

"And she's looking for a part-time job," Abbott added. "She

recently retired from her administrative job at MUSC, but she doesn't know what to do with so much time on her hands."

"Hmm." Ellie scrunched up her eyebrows in thought. "That could work. Lacey could set her own hours. She could manage the big-picture operations, including hiring whatever staff we need to greet the public." Ellie winked at her father. "I'll talk to her when you bring her to the girls' birthday party."

Julian clapped his hands. "Okay then! It's almost time to eat. Girls, why don't you put away your coloring things, and help Aunt Ellie set the table."

The twins gathered their coloring books and crayons, and carried them to the alcove beside the back door, where Julian had designed a bench and cabinetry with cubbyholes for their coats, shoes, and toys. A warm glow settled over Ellie as they gathered around the table for their first meal together in their new kitchen. At long last, her grandmother's house felt like home. Aside from converting the utility room to a powder room, the major renovations were complete. The roof no longer leaked, and every exterior and interior wall sported a new coat of paint. Jackie was still working on a few accents, but most of the draperies, wallpaper, rugs, and furniture were in place. The walls remained bare, however. Much to her husband's chagrin, Ellie preferred to sell her own work. Only two paintings adorned her walls—the contemporary piece on the fireplace in Julian's study, and an acrylic on canvas that hung above the console table in the center hallway. The latter, which featured a magnolia blossom, she'd purchased from a gallery showing her first week in town. The magnolia held special meaning for Ellie. Not only had she met Julian while admiring the painting at the exhibit, the subject matter reminded her of the long hours she'd spent under the tree as a child. The magnolia painting was the first in the collection she hoped to build of contemporary works from local artists.

Julian and Abbott tackled the dishes while Ellie took the girls upstairs for their bath. While the twins splashed in the tub, she left the door open so she could keep an eye on them as she roamed from bedroom to bedroom, making notes of the small details that still needed to be addressed—a valance of some sort for the window in the room the twins shared, fabric for the chaise lounge in the master bedroom, and decorative pillows for the queen bed in Katie's room. They planned to convert one of the two spares into a nursery and to use the remaining bedroom for guests, if they ever had any.

Ellie had decided a long time ago that if and when her sister returned to town, she would put her up in one of the area's many charming inns. The last time her sister had stayed in the house with them, back in September, she'd taken up residence in Ellie's bedroom and refused to move to the guest room despite Ellie's numerous hints. Now that she was a suspect in her husband's murder, she no longer trusted Lia enough to sleep under the same roof with her or the twins.

She tucked the twins in and read them two bedtime stories. When she went back downstairs, forty-five minutes later, she found Abbott and Julian drinking cognac on the terrace outside. She smiled to herself at the sight of their heads close together in deep conversation. Her husband and father had become instant friends when they met last fall, and that friendship had deepened during the months that followed.

She brewed a cup of tea and joined them. "What are y'all talking about so secretively out here?" she asked, taking a seat in the chair beside Julian.

Abbott cleared his throat. "We were talking about Lia. Have you heard anything from the detective in Key West?"

"Not a word," Ellie said. "I'm trying not to think about it."

Julian said, "I told your dad, and I could be wrong, but I don't think we're ever going to see your sister again."

"I hate to admit it, but that would probably be best for everyone involved." Ellie let her head fall against the back of the chair. The night sky was bright with stars, and the air was crisp and clean. She inhaled a deep breath. "Hmm . . . Don't you love the citrusy-sweet fragrance of magnolia blossoms? My life had little structure when I lived here as a child. When you're kept in a house like a prisoner, one day feels the same as the next. But during the summer, when the days were long, I was allowed to stay outside until nearly bedtime. The blooming of the magnolia tree in late spring was promise that those longer days were ahead."

They sat in silence for a few minutes, each of them lost in their own thoughts while they finished their drinks.

Finally, Abbott stood and stretched. "I need to get home to bed. I have an early day tomorrow."

"I'll walk you out," Ellie said, rising out of her chair.

At the door, Abbott took her by the shoulders and kissed her on the forehead. "I'm so happy for you, sweetheart. You're gonna be a wonderful mother for your baby, just as you've been for the twins. Thanks for a wonderful evening and for allowing me to share your life."

"Thank you, Daddy. I can't bring myself to think about what my life would've been like without you."

Ellie closed the door behind him and leaned against it. She'd come so close to not having a father. She could very well have ended up like her sister, pawned off on some lunatic woman who knew nothing about raising children. Her father had rescued her from this house. He'd nurtured her out of the darkness and taught her how to live in the real world.

ELLIE

*E*llie jolted upright in bed at the shrill ringing of her cell phone. The amber digits of her alarm clock on the bedside table read 3:15. She snatched up her phone and accepted the call. A tiny voice whimpered her name. Ellie's heart beat in her throat. She knew without a doubt the distraught person on the other end was Ruby. Both feet hit the ground with a thump.

"Ruby, is that you?" she asked in a low, desperate voice.

"Please help me, Mrs. Hagood," Ruby murmured. "He's coming to get me. He's breaking into my room."

"Who is he, Ruby?" Ellie asked as she struggled into the yoga pants and T-shirt she'd set out for her early morning walk.

"My mother's boyfriend!"

Ignoring Julian's eyes on her, Ellie punched the code on the panel beside her bedroom door that disengaged the security system. "I'm calling the police, Ruby honey, and I'm on my way. Is there somewhere you can hide until we get there?" she asked as she flew down the stairs.

"Hurry! He's beating down the door."

Ellie heard the sound of loud banging on Ruby's end of the

line. "Where are you now?" she asked as she frantically searched the downstairs for her purse.

"In my closet," she sniffled.

"Listen carefully, Ruby. I'm going to call the police from my landline, but I'm not going to hang up on you. While I'm talking to the police, I want you to stay in your closet and try not to cry. Close your eyes and think of a song you really like. Hum it in your head if it helps."

"I'm scared," Ruby moaned.

The line went dead.

"Ruby! Ruby, are you still there?"

The line remained silent.

Ellie looked up to see Julian watching her from the doorway of the kitchen. "It's Ruby. Her mother's boyfriend is threatening her. I've gotta get to her."

"Call the police and let them handle it," he said in a deadpan tone.

"I'm calling them now." She punched 9-1-1 into her keypad and held her phone out to him as evidence.

He moved toward her, and she backed away from him. "I'm sorry, Julian. I have to go. This child needs me. I promise I'll be careful."

"Then I'll go with you. Give me a minute to get some clothes on."

"Someone has to stay here with the girls."

"Right. I'm calling Abbot," he said, his phone already pressed to his ear. "Text me the address. I'll meet you there as soon as he gets here."

She grabbed her purse from the bench beside the back door. Then she clicked the button on her way to the car and put the call through to 9-1-1. As she fumbled with her car keys, she explained the situation to the operator. The nasal voice responded, "The incident has already been reported, and the police have been dispatched."

She felt an immediate sense of relief at knowing the police were already on the way. After texting the address to Julian, she put the car in reverse and backed out of the driveway. As she zipped through the sleeping streets of Charleston, she tried to reconnect with Ruby multiple times, but it went straight to her mother's voice mail. When Ellie rounded the corner onto Ruby's street, she spotted Marta standing with a small group of ten or twelve onlookers watching the incident unfold at the Fuquas' home. Ellie parked on the curb, as close as she could get to the scene, and joined Marta on the sidewalk.

"When did the police get here?" Ellie asked.

"A few minutes ago. I called them when I heard loud voices and what I thought sounded like gunfire, although I'm not a hundred percent sure it *was* gunfire."

A young policewoman, Officer Cummings according to her badge, motioned the onlookers to move away from the yellow tape. They stepped back as instructed and watched, transfixed, as the policemen busted down the front door.

When Marta leaned in close, Ellie caught a whiff of Noxzema night cream that summoned a flashback of her mother.

"How did you know to come?" Marta asked.

"Ruby called me about twenty minutes ago. Her mother's boyfriend was banging down the door to her bedroom. She was terrified, hiding out in the closet."

Marta's hand flew to her mouth. "Oh dear."

Ellie held her phone tight with her left hand in case Ruby called again. They waited for the police to emerge. Fifteen minutes passed before two officers exited the house escorting suspects in handcuffs—a woman and a man. Ruby's mother's face was bruised and bloody, her bleached hair a rat's nest. The officers shoved their prisoners in separate patrol cars. One of the officers barked at a nearby coworker, "Get the Drug Task Force in here! There's enough meth in that house to get the population of Texas high."

They heard the sound of an ambulance in the distance. Within seconds, flashing red lights lit up the dark street. "Who's the ambulance for?" Marta asked. "Do you think they're coming for Ruby?"

Ellie's stomach lurched. "I pray not."

A crew of three EMTs piled out of the ambulance and jogged across the dirt yard to the house. Overcome by nausea, Ellie excused herself from the group and vomited in the shrubbery near Marta's house. Julian was waiting for her on the sidewalk when she rejoined the onlookers.

Placing an arm around her, he gave her a half squeeze. "Where were you? I was worried. I saw your car, but couldn't find you anywhere."

"Throwing up in the bushes."

He peered at her from under furrowed eyebrows. "Are you serious?"

"Yes, I'm serious, Julian. I'm scared to death for that child."

As the words left her lips, an EMT appeared in the doorway, carrying a child in his arms.

"Stay here. I don't want you to scare her." Ellie left Julian standing on the sidewalk. She crossed the street, shrugging off Officer Cummings when she tried to stop her. Ruby caught sight of Ellie and struggled free of the rescue worker. Keeping her left arm close to her body, she ran to Ellie, planted her face in her belly, and sobbed.

Ellie wrapped her arms around Ruby and held the child's trembling body tight. "You're okay now, sweetheart. It's over. Nobody's going to hurt you anymore."

Officer Cummings approached them. "Are you a relative?"

Ellie shook her head. "I'm one of her teachers."

"We need to contact a family member. Does she have any that you know of?"

"Ruby, honey," she whispered into the child's hair. "You need to calm down so we can help you. Let's take some deep breaths."

Ellie counted out loud as they inhaled and exhaled together. Ruby slowly gained control of her emotions, and her sobbing subsided.

"There, now. That's better." Ellie tilted Ruby's chin up so she could see her face. "Tell me, sweetheart, do you have any family nearby? Your grandmother maybe, or your father?"

Fresh tears welled up in her wide green eyes. "No, ma'am. My father died when I was a baby, and I don't have any grandparents. Mama's the only family I got."

Officer Cummings bent over to be at eye level with Ruby. "Are you hurt, sweetheart?"

"Yes, ma'am. My arm and my face." Ruby lifted her fingers to the bloody gash on her cheek.

"Can you tell me what happened to your arm?" Cummings asked.

Ruby bit down on her lip in an effort to stop it from quivering. "He was beating my mama. When I tried to make him stop, he smacked me away. I twisted my arm when I fell."

"We should let the EMTs have a look." Cummings gestured at the crew waiting at the back of the ambulance.

With her good arm, Ruby gripped Ellie's leg and refused to let go. "Don't worry, Ruby," Cummings said. "Your teacher can come with us."

The threesome walked together to the ambulance. One of the EMTs asked Ruby several questions about her arm while another blotted the wound on her face with a gauze pad.

Ellie pulled Cummings aside. "What's going to happen to her?"

"Social Services will try to locate her relatives. If none can be found, she will be placed in foster care."

Based on what Ruby had told them, Ellie doubted if any relatives existed. Her heart broke for the little girl sitting in the back of the ambulance. Day after day, Ruby had come to school with a bright smile on her sweet face—when all the while she was experiencing such atrocities at home. What kind of mother allowed her boyfriend to abuse her child? In this case, the answer was obvious—a woman addicted to meth, who didn't deserve the privilege of being a mother.

Ellie and Julian followed the ambulance to MUSC in Ellie's car. They stayed with Ruby while she was treated in the pediatric emergency room. The doctor saw no evidence of sexual abuse, but scars and faded bruises on her pale body suggested a history of physical abuse. He stitched up the laceration on her face, and when the X-rays confirmed his suspicion of a dislocated shoulder, he returned the bone to its correct position and placed her arm in a sling. Ruby, exhausted by the time it was all over, went willingly with the Social Services' on-call worker whose job was to find a place for Ruby to sleep that night.

Ellie and Julian followed them out to the parking lot. "I'd like to talk to the person who will be in charge of Ruby's case going forward," she said to the on-call worker. "Do you know who that will be?"

The young woman pressed a business card in Ellie's hand. "Call this number during business hours and ask to speak to the social worker handling her case."

The rising sun was casting a rosy glow on the clouds as they made their way back to the Fuquas' street to pick up Julian's car.

"What a night," Julian said as they walked in the back door at home.

She set her bag down on the bench. "I feel so sorry for that poor child. She told me she has only her mother, no other family. She's all alone in the world."

He sank to a nearby barstool. "What are you plotting, Ellie? I can tell something is brewing in your mind."

She made herself a cup of lemon-ginger tea and stood at the counter beside him. "We have to help her, Julian. I can't just turn my back on her."

"And just how do you plan on helping her?"

"I'd like for us to be her foster parents."

"I don't know, honey," he said, shaking his head. "That sounds like a huge commitment, especially when we already have two foster children asleep upstairs." He pointed at the ceiling.

"Bella and Mya are not my foster children. They're my nieces, my family. Once the adoption goes through, they will legally be our daughters."

"And what about Ruby? Sounds like her mother will be going to jail for a long time. You'll be satisfied with the foster relationship for a while, but you'll soon want to adopt her as well."

She rested a hand on his shoulder. "Would that be so terrible, Julian? She's an enthusiastic child with the potential to make something of herself, and we have the means to provide for her. Lately I've had this feeling that I inherited my grandmother's estate for a reason. I believe God has something special planned for this house. I've always wanted a family of my own—"

He stood to face her. "Need I remind you that you're pregnant? You're about to have that family."

"There's plenty of room and money for all the children—our baby, the twins, Ruby. We're blessed with this opportunity."

"Don't forget I have a daughter, too." Julian's face was flushed with anger. "Where does Katie fit in? She's struggling at home, and she needs my support right now. Don't make me choose between my own flesh and blood and your foster children."

Her eyebrows shot up. "What's that supposed to mean?"

"It means . . . I don't know what it means, Ellie. Let's go to bed." He removed her teacup from her hand and set it down on the table. "We've had a long night. We can talk more about this tomorrow. I'm sure if we put our heads together, we can come up with a way to help Ruby."

ELLIE

*J*ulian was snoring by the time Ellie emerged from the bathroom. But she couldn't sleep for worrying about Ruby. When she heard the pitter-patter of little feet in the hallway, she got up and followed the twins to the kitchen. Maddie was already working on the promised waffles.

She jiggled her spatula at Ellie. "I'll get started on your breakfast hash, Miss Ellie, as soon as I get these young'uns fed."

"Thanks, Maddie, but I'm not feeling well this morning. I don't think I could stomach a bite."

Maddie furrowed her brows. "You ain't getting sick on me now, are ya? You need a spoonful of cod liver oil. Always did the trick when you was little."

The color drained from Ellie's face. "No, thank you." A surge of dizziness overcame her as she gripped the edge of the countertop. "If you don't mind watching the twins, I need to go lie down."

Julian was shaving when she returned to their room. She lay down on the bed, closed her eyes, and this time fell fast asleep. When she came back downstairs two hours later, showered and dressed and ready to discuss Ruby's future with her husband, she was disappointed to see his study door closed. They'd argued before over issues related to household management, but not over anything of importance. He'd never issued an ultimatum.

"Don't make me choose between my own flesh and blood and your foster children," he'd said.

She understood she was asking a lot of him. Being a foster parent was an enormous commitment. But they'd been blessed with so much.

What is so wrong with wanting to share our good fortune?

Becca had taken the twins to a program for young children at the aquarium. Desperate for a distraction, Ellie drove her car to the gallery. She circled the block several times before she located a parking place two streets over. Much progress had been made during her seven-day absence from the gallery. The project would be complete in another week or so. But the walls would remain bare. There was no art to hang. There was no desk where the gallery manager would sit. There was no gallery manager.

Her father was working night and day to get his photographs ready for the showing. But she needed more than his collection. There were plenty of local artists with available work to exhibit. Unfortunately, she knew none of them. She didn't have the luxury of waiting until the twins' birthday party to find out if Lacey was interested in the job. She would get her phone number from Julian and call her right away.

She left the banging and sawing in the showroom downstairs and climbed the iron stairs to her studio. She stared out across the rooftops of the downtown buildings, to the harbor. A sense of dread for the uncertain future settled in her gut.

What will become of Ruby? And the twins? And Katie?

With Julian's support, they could be one big, happy family if all went well with the court system. She'd been single all her life —with the exception of the last six months. She wasn't used to anyone dictating her decisions. She loved Julian with all her heart, but she couldn't turn her back on Ruby. Julian had told her to do what she had to do. And she would. She couldn't live with her conscience otherwise.

She dug the business card the social worker had given her out of her bag and placed the call to Social Services. She was transferred four times without success. No one there had ever heard of Ruby Fuqua.

I'll go visit them in person. It'll be harder for them to put me off face-to-face.

She spoke to the workmen on her way out of the gallery and promised to have her decorator select the paint colors they'd requested. She keyed the address into her map app and followed the voice directions to the Department of Social Services, on the north side of town. When the receptionist—a woman about Ellie's age with deep lines in her forehead from scowling—attempted to give Ellie the runaround, she demanded to see the supervisor in charge.

"Take a seat." The receptionist motioned her to the waiting room. "She'll be with you as soon as possible."

Ellie watched the seconds tick by on the wall clock. It felt like five hours, but it was only twenty minutes before the receptionist directed her to the last office down the hall on the right.

Beth Morgan greeted her at the door. Her sparkling blue eyes and gentle smile instilled trust in Ellie.

They sat down across from each other at her desk. "I'm not at liberty to divulge any information about her temporary placement, but I can tell you Ruby is being well taken care of. The first step in the process is locating her relatives. So far, we haven't had any luck." Beth explained that her department's main objective was reuniting children with their parents. "The chances of that happening in Ruby's case are slim, considering the drug charges her mother faces. She most certainly will do jail time, quite a lot of it according to my source at the Charleston PD."

"I'd like to apply to be her foster parent," Ellie said. "I care about Ruby, and I have the means to provide for her. I can offer her a loving and safe home."

"Really?" Beth said, her blue eyes peering at Ellie over the top of her tortoiseshell reading glasses. "How does your husband feel about this?"

Ellie hesitated. "He has some reservations, but he'll come around. Julian is a kind man and a wonderful father."

"With all due respect, Mrs. Hagood, people don't *come around* to being a foster parent. It takes a special kind of person. Foster parenting isn't for everyone. You're either committed or you're not. Raising a child as your own only to have that child taken away from you years down the road can be traumatic."

Ellie's chest tightened at the thought of losing a child she loved. She was already in that predicament with the twins. She shrugged off her doubt. She couldn't think about "down the road." Ruby needed her now.

"I know my husband. Julian will come around once he's had a chance to think about it."

"You should be aware, Mrs. Hagood, that we'll be conducting a background check and home inspection. If either of you are hiding anything, we'll know about it."

Ellie's mind raced.

Is there anything in my or Julian's past that would prevent us from being approved? What about his divorce? What if they learn my sister is a murder suspect and that I'm currently taking care of my sister's children? Would they consider my home an unsafe place knowing my sister, who could possibly be dangerous, might show up at any time?

She straightened. She would cross that bridge when she got to it. "As I said a minute ago, Ms. Morgan, I'm confident in our ability to provide a loving home for Ruby. I'm ready to proceed."

Beth got up from her desk and went to a metal file cabinet behind her. She opened the top drawer, removed a sheaf of papers, and handed it to Ellie. "Why don't you take the paperwork with you? That way you and your husband can fill it out together."

"Is there somewhere I can fill out my portion while I'm here? The sooner the better, right?"

"I'll show you to a room down the hall if you'd like to take care of it now."

Ellie gulped. Her stomach was tied up in knots.

How will I get Julian to fill out his paperwork when he seemed so opposed to being a foster parent?

She pressed her hand to her belly. "There's a child desperately in need of a home. I'd like to get my paperwork in as soon as possible."

Ellie followed Beth to a small, windowless room down the hall.

"I'm due in a meeting," she said. "When you're finished with the paperwork, you can leave it with my assistant. You understand I can't proceed until I receive your husband's paperwork."

"I understand. After Julian gets his paperwork in, how soon should we expect to hear from you?"

"Within a day or two. It's in the child's best interest to find her permanent placement as soon as possible. I've spoken to Ruby. She trusts you. I'll do everything in my power to make this placement happen."

She's spoken to Ruby about me? Ellie thought. *Why didn't she mention that earlier? Was she testing me?*

Ellie held her tongue and smiled her thanks. After Beth left the room, she sat staring at the blank forms. This was the right decision for Ruby, but what about everyone else involved? The twins would surely love having a nine-year-old in their lives just as much as they loved having Katie.

But what about Julian? Am I willing to risk our marriage for this child?

If he chose not to support Ellie in this, he wasn't the man she thought she'd married. Forcing thoughts of her husband from her mind, she set pen to paper and filled out the forms. By the time she'd finished, the uncertainty had returned, even stronger than before.

She gathered up the papers, marched them down the hall, and handed them to Beth's assistant.

She was almost to her car when she felt a stabbing pain in her gut—a pain that had nothing to do with Ruby or Julian or Social Services. Another pain gripped her abdomen, and she doubled over, feeling warm liquid between her legs.

Oh my god! This can't be happening, she thought.

Staggering to the car, she fumbled with her keys, unlocked the door, and started the engine. She was way across town. She had two choices—either call 9-1-1 or drive herself to the hospital. She removed her phone from her bag. When she received her husband's voice mail, she called her father.

"Oh god, Daddy," she cried when Abbott answered the phone. "I think I'm having a miscarriage."

"Where are you, honey?" he said in the calm voice that had guided her through the years.

"In North Charleston." She grabbed hold of the steering wheel as pain tore through her belly and radiated throughout her body.

"Are you able to drive yourself to the hospital?"

"I'll get there somehow." She threw her car in gear. "My doctor's name is Ellen Gillespie. Call her office and tell her staff I'm on my way to Roper Hospital."

"I'll take care of it, honey. Unless you hear back from me, I'll meet you at the emergency room. Do you want me to call Julian for you?"

"If you can reach him. I tried, but I got his voice mail."

Ellie was grateful when he didn't press her with questions.

She white-knuckled the steering wheel with her right hand and pressed her left hand against her abdomen as she maneuvered the Mini onto the highway and back toward downtown. The pains were coming fast, and blood had seeped through the crotch of her khaki slacks by the time she arrived at the emergency room. As promised, her father was waiting for her on the sidewalk out front. She parked in a handicapped space as Abbott hurried over with a wheelchair to assist her. Inside the emergency room, he turned Ellie over to a triage nurse.

He knelt down beside her. "Julian's on his way."

Her eyes filled with tears that spilled down her cheeks. "He warned me not to push too hard, but I didn't listen. I'm losing our baby, and it's all my fault."

ELLIE

*J*ulian arrived at the hospital within minutes of Abbott calling him. He remained at Ellie's bedside throughout the horrific ordeal. He wiped her forehead with a cool washcloth, held her hand, and whispered comforting words near her ear. The hurt in his eyes was apparent when the doctor cautioned Ellie about trying to get pregnant again.

"Because of your age, your chances of carrying a healthy baby to term are slim," Dr. Gillespie said. "You might consider other options, like adoption."

But Ellie knew no adoption agency would give a newborn to a forty-year-old woman when millions of younger couples were waiting in line to adopt.

She was released from the emergency room around midnight on Thursday night. She rode home with Julian in his SUV. They didn't speak during the short drive, and when they arrived at the house on South Battery, he helped her up the stairs to the second floor. The guest bedroom door was open, her father's loud snores coming from within. Julian went to their room to start the shower for her while she tiptoed across the hall to check on the girls. Bella and Mya were sleeping peacefully, with their limbs tangled together in their queen-size bed. Ellie had tried to convince them to trade their queen bed in for twins, but they'd refused. Maddie, who'd stayed over to help Abbott with the girls, slept on the daybed in the adjoining room, her mouth slack and her arms across her chest.

Ellie stripped off her clothes in the en-suite bathroom and stepped into the shower. The hot water massaged her aching body and rinsed away all traces of her hospital stay. In the solitude of her shower stall, she was able to finally release the emotions she'd been holding back for the past twelve hours. Dropping to her knees on the marble floor, she bit down on her balled fist and rocked back and forth as she sobbed. She cried until her skin was pink, her fingers pruned, and her well of emotions empty. She slipped into her robe and wrapped her wet hair in a towel. The covers were turned back, but her bed was empty when she emerged from the bathroom. She assumed Julian was letting the dogs out, and she sat on the side of the bed for a long time waiting for him to return. Finally, her aching body got the best of her and she slid beneath the cool covers of her bed. She closed her eyes, but the burden of guilt weighed heavily on her, preventing her from falling asleep.

My greed ruined everything.

Before she moved to Charleston, she'd all but given up on having a family of her own. The stars had aligned for her when she met Julian and they'd gotten pregnant two months after their wedding. Instead of prioritizing her health and the fetus growing inside her womb, she'd pushed herself by renovating her house and art gallery, flying off to Key West to look for her sister, and getting involved with Ruby's problems at home.

I blew my one chance to have a baby of my own. Will Julian ever forgive me?

She'd seen the pain etched in his face. She didn't blame him if he didn't. She was certain she'd never forgive herself.

For the rest of the night, she lay in the dark, curled in a fetal position, reliving the events of the past months over and over in her mind while waiting for Julian to come to bed. Daylight finally peeked through the blinds, but the dawn of a new day offered no sign of her husband and no consolation to her grief. Not even when she heard the other occupants of the house moving about in the hall outside her room or when she heard her father shushing the twins.

"Aunt Ellie is sleeping," he said. "She was up late last night. Let's not disturb her."

Sometime later, perhaps an hour, maybe longer, someone tapped lightly on the door and Maddie entered her room with a breakfast tray. "Morning, baby. I thought you might be getting hungry."

Ellie usually liked it when Maddie called her "baby." It made her feel loved when Maddie fussed over her as a small child. But today, her term of endearment echoed throughout the empty room and brought fresh tears to her eyes.

"Oh, honey." Maddie set the breakfast tray on the bedside table and sat down on the bed beside her. "I know you're hurting. Ain't nothing gonna take away the pain but time."

"My life is over," Ellie sobbed. "Not only did I lose the baby, I've lost Julian as well."

Maddie's brown eyes grew large. "What makes you think you done lost Mr. Julian?"

"He blames me for the miscarriage, and he's right. It's all my fault. I should've taken better care of myself."

"You hush that crazy talk now." Maddie massaged her leg through the comforter. "Nobody blames you for losing the baby. Sometimes Mother Nature gets it wrong. It's as simple as that. Mr. Julian adores you as much as he adores them little girls. Just like they were his own flesh and blood. Experiencing a loss like this helps us see all the good things we have in our lives. And you have plenty to be thankful for—a beautiful home and family. You have to be strong for the twins. They need you."

Ellie struggled to sit up in bed. "That's just it, though, Maddie. Lia could show up at any minute and take them away from me. Then I'll have nobody left."

"Bella and Mya ain't going nowhere. For all we know, Lia done got herself killed along with their daddy. You gone get to keep them little girls. I feel it in my bones."

Ellie threw back the covers and eased her sore body off the other side of the bed. She went to the window and watched a group of small children playing in the park. Their mothers gathered in a circle nearby, chatting and sipping coffee, as if without a care in the world. A woman standing nearby, who looked eerily like her sister, noticed Ellie in the window and waved at her.

"You know what I feel in my bones, Maddie? Like Lia's out there somewhere, watching and waiting for the right time to swoop in and take the girls away."

Maddie joined her at the window. "You tired, baby. And rightly so. Ain't nobody out there watching you."

"Then explain why every good thing that's ever happened to me in my life has gone bad. I'm poison to everyone I've ever cared about."

"You better not let your daddy hear you talking like that. I've never seen a man love his daughter the way Mr. Abbott loves you."

"What about my mother? If not for me, she'd still be alive."

"You talking nonsense, baby. You were just a wee child at the time. You had nothing to do with her dying. Your gramma's the one to blame. If she'd taken your mama to see the doctor, she'd still be alive." She wrapped her arm around Ellie and squeezed her tight. "You've been through a terrible ordeal. You need time to heal. You'll feel better in a couple of days."

"You're wrong, Maddie. My heart is not strong enough to recover from this. I don't know how I'll ever be able to move on."

"You live one moment at the time. That's how. When you feel like it, you eat some food. When you have your strength back, whether that's today or the next day or next week, you put on some clothes, brush your hair, and face the world. Your heart is full of love, Miss Ellie Pringle Hagood. And there are plenty of people who need that love. I know from experience that you don't have to birth a baby from your body to love it like your own. I ain't never told you this, but you the one who saved me from my own heartache."

Ellie furrowed her brow. "What do you mean?"

Maddie walked her back to the bed and pulled her down to the mattress beside her. "I understand a little about what you're going through. I had my share of miscarriages, round about the time you were living here with your grandmother. Eight of them, if anyone's counting. I never carried a one of them to term. I never had my own baby, but I had you. And you needed me. We needed each other. You gave me the strength to face each day."

Ellie stared at Maddie. "I don't understand. I've heard you talk about your children before."

"They ain't my own, though. Henry and Joshua are my sister's boys. About ten years after you went to live with your father, my sister's husband beat her to death. Leroy went to prison, and her sons came to live with me. They were just boys at the time. Leroy died in prison a year later, and I was able to raise them as my own." She took Ellie's hands in hers. "Losing you was the worst thing that ever happened to me, but having you back in my life is the best. Nothing in this life comes without risk, Miss Ellie. But if you don't take the risk, you don't get the reward. You eventually came back to me. And that is my reward."

ELLIE

llie sent the breakfast tray back to the kitchen with Maddie and turned her nose up at the homemade chicken-noodle soup the housekeeper brought her for lunch. She pretended to be asleep when Julian came in to shower and dress for an afternoon meeting with his new client, and when the twins peeked through the cracked door to check on her. But she could no longer ignore the hunger pangs gnawing at her stomach when Maddie delivered her tea tray—a cup of raspberry brew, three tiny cucumber sandwiches, and two cheese straws—around four o'clock. She hadn't eaten a proper meal since breakfast the previous morning.

"You eat now, baby," Maddie said, brushing her hair out of her face. "You need the nourishment to get your strength back. I left a platter of fried chicken and buttermilk biscuits warming in the oven for your dinner. I hope you don't mind if I head home a few minutes early this evening." She lifted her fingers to her cropped gray head. "I must look a sight after sleeping in my clothes all night."

Ellie gave a smile, her first since the miscarriage. "You look as lovely as ever. I appreciate you staying with Dad last night." She took a bite of a cheese straw. "The house is so quiet. Where is everyone? Has Julian come home yet?"

"No'm, the house is empty. Mr. Julian's still out at his meeting, and the twins are at the park with Becca. Your daddy has gone on a photo shoot, but he's planning to come back for dinner. He said for you to call him if you need anything beforehand." She moved to the door. "I done loaded up the refrigerator for the weekend. You shouldn't have to go to the store till I come back on Monday." She gripped the door handle. "I feel bad about leaving you in this condition, Miss Ellie. I can come in tomorrow if you want."

Ellie shook her head. "Thanks for the offer, but you go and enjoy your weekend with your family. Julian and I will manage fine."

"Okay, then. But you call me if you need me," she said, wagging her finger at Ellie. "I'll be here right away."

As she watched Maddie limp off down the hall, Ellie wondered how much longer the old woman would be able to work. She planned to provide for her housekeeper in her retirement, but she would miss having her around.

While she finished her snack, she thought about the things the housekeeper had confided earlier in the day. How had Maddie survived eight miscarriages?

If you don't take the risk, you don't get the reward.

Ellie would avoid getting pregnant again. Even if she was able to carry the fetus to term, the risk of birth defects was too great. And that was not the kind of risk she was willing to take.

But what about the risk involved with adopting the twins?

What if I take that risk and lose? What if the judge denies my request for adoption? What if Lia shows up as suddenly as she disappeared?

She was already risking heartache, but not by choice. She couldn't throw the twins out on the street. But she could do a better job of protecting her heart. She would withdraw her petition for legal guardianship. She would take care of the girls until their mother returned.

I can do that without becoming more emotionally involved than I already am. Can't I?

Ellie placed the tray on the mattress beside her and lay back against the mountain of feather pillows. She was dozing off when the doorbell rang. She pulled the covers over her head, hoping whoever it was would go away, but when the bell rang again—followed by the clanging of the knocker—she forced herself to get out of bed and go answer it.

A young woman with sea-green eyes and a creamy complexion stood in the doorway. "I'm Franny Flowers from the Department of Social Services, here to see Eleanor Hagood."

Ellie drew her robe tighter around her body. "I'm Ellie Hagood. I'm sorry, I wasn't expecting you."

"That's the point of our surprise home inspections, Mrs. Hagood. Popping in unannounced gives us a better understanding of your lifestyle." The social worker gave her a quick once-over, starting and ending at her bare feet.

Ellie's mind raced as she considered how much to tell her. She hated sharing her personal business with a total stranger, and she shuddered to think what this woman must think of her disheveled appearance.

"I apologize for my appearance, Ms. Flowers. I don't usually lie around in my bathrobe all day. I suffered a miscarriage last night."

The woman pressed her fingers to her lips. "Oh, you poor dear. I'm so sorry. I'll come back another time."

She started to turn away, but Ellie stopped her. "Don't go! I assume you are here about Ruby."

The woman nodded, and Ellie opened the door wider. "Please! Won't you come in?"

She hesitated. "Are you sure, Mrs. Hagood? I can come back on Monday."

"I'm positive. It's important that we talk." She extended her hand to the woman. "And call me Ellie."

The woman took Ellie's hand. "Nice to meet you, Ellie. I'm Franny."

"Why don't we talk in the kitchen?" Ellie said, ushering her guest down the hall to the back of the house. "Can I offer you a glass of sweet tea?"

"Tea would be lovely."

Ellie poured two glasses of tea and handed one to Franny. They sat down across from each other at the kitchen table.

"I've been assigned to Ruby's case," Franny said as she opened a file. "Beth Morgan spoke highly of you when we met earlier today. Considering your . . . um . . . loss, you may want to withdraw or postpone your application to be Ruby's foster parent."

Ellie ran her fingers through her matted hair and tied it back with an elastic tie from her wrist. "I appreciate your concern, but I'll be fine in a day or two. I want what's best for Ruby. I'll let the Department of Social Services determine what that is."

"We feel that placing a child with relatives is usually the best option. However, in Ruby's case, after an extensive search, we've been unable to locate any family members." Franny went on to talk about the application process and the pros and cons of foster parenting. "I'll be honest with you. Being a foster parent is not for the faint of heart. You need to be prepared for a difficult transition. I'm not saying this is the case with Ruby, but many times these children experience symptoms of post-traumatic stress disorder brought about by the atrocities they suffered in their own homes. And it's my understanding that Ruby was physically abused."

Ellie grimaced at the thought of anyone hurting her little friend. "Ruby is an enthusiastic, intelligent child who deserves so much more than she's been given. I'm prepared to support her in every way." Ellie couldn't believe her own ears. An hour ago, she'd made a vow to herself to protect her heart.

Franny shuffled the papers in her file. "I trust your husband feels the same way. I'd like to speak with him. And we need his paperwork. Is he here?"

"He's not home at the moment. He's an architect and is meeting with clients. I'm not sure when he'll be back."

"I won't be able to complete my portion of the application process until I speak with him," Franny said with a glance at her watch. "Are you up for giving me a tour of the house while we wait? I'd like to see where Ruby will sleep."

Ellie hadn't given any thought to where Ruby would sleep. She explained her recent renovations as she walked Franny through the downstairs. When they moved to the second floor, she showed her the two spare bedrooms, saying she would fix whichever one Ruby chose to her liking.

"You have a lovely home with enough rooms to house an army of foster children." She circled the upstairs, pausing in the doorway of each bedroom. "Oh!" she exclaimed when they reached the twins' bedroom. "I didn't realize you have other children."

"Bella and Mya are my nieces. My sister left them in my care. It's a complicated situation." Ellie offered a brief explanation as to how the twins had come to live with her.

"In the nontechnical sense, you already are a foster parent. I'd like to meet Bella and Mya."

"They're with the babysitter in the park across the street. I can call—"

The slamming of the front door followed by the squeaking of sneakers and clicking of paws on the hardwood floor finished her sentence.

"You're in luck. Sounds like they just got home."

They found the twins slurping on Capri Sun juice pouches at the counter in the kitchen. The knees of their blue jeans were grass stained, and their faces smeared with dirt.

"Looks like someone had a good time in the park." Ellie,

feeling no obligation to provide a reason for the social worker's visit, said, "Becca, girls, I'd like you to meet my friend Franny."

For the next few minutes, Franny quizzed them about their lives in a friendly manner, as a teacher might her students, interrogating them without them realizing they were being interrogated. When the girls had finished their juices, Becca took them upstairs for an early bath.

"They're adorable," Franny said. "I know how hard it will be for you to give them up when their mother returns."

Spoken like a true social worker, Ellie thought as she swallowed the lump in her throat.

Watching caring parents give up children they loved was an everyday occurrence for Franny.

Am I doing the right thing? Is it possible for her to provide for Ruby without giving her a piece of my heart? Then again, haven't I already given Ruby a piece of my heart? Isn't that what this was all about?

"You have a wonderful family, Ellie. I know Ruby will be very happy here."

She was gathering up her file when Julian came through the back door. Franny crossed the room with an outstretched hand.

"I'm Franny Flowers, with the Department of Social Services. I'm sure you've had a long day, but if I may have a moment of your time, I'd like to talk to you about your application to foster Ruby Fuqua."

Julian's jaw tightened, but to his credit, his smile remained intact. "I wasn't aware we'd gotten to the application phase, but okay."

"Does that mean you're opposed to being a foster parent, Mr. Hagood?"

He set his briefcase down on the bench beside the back door. "It means the timing isn't great."

"I understand, sir. And I'm sorry for your loss." Franny paused a moment before continuing. "Based on a preliminary review of your application, your credentials exceed our expectations. We'd like to place Ruby in your home as soon as possible, but we can't proceed without your paperwork."

"I haven't seen any paperwork, Ms. Flowers."

"I started miscarrying on my way home from Beth's office yesterday," Ellie explained. "I haven't had a chance to give it to him yet."

"Of course you haven't. I'm so sorry," she said to Ellie as she turned to Julian. "For both of you. This is a difficult time for you. I told your wife earlier, considering the circumstances, I wouldn't blame you if you wanted to postpone the application."

"That would probably be best," Julian said. "At least for a few days."

ELLIE

"Julian, I can explain," Ellie said, closing the door behind Franny after seeing her out.

His hand shot out. "Save it, Ellie. No explanation could possibly justify your actions. You've never been married before, so I can see why you don't understand how these things work. You knew I had reservations about being a foster parent, yet you took it upon yourself to proceed with the application. Fostering a child is a big emotional and financial commitment. We have to give it careful consideration to decide if it's the right thing for everyone in this family."

They stood, glaring at each other in the hallway, their bodies rigid with tension. "I admit I may have acted in haste. But I wasn't trying to go behind your back. I was on my way home from Social Services yesterday to talk to you about being Ruby's foster parents and to give you your portion of the paperwork when I had the miscarriage. Please, won't you at least consider it? Ruby needs me. She needs us. I can't just turn my back on her."

"There are three other people in this house who need you, Ellie. Our unborn baby needed you."

His words stung, and she took a step backward as though

she'd been slapped. "That's not fair, and you know it." She placed her hand on her belly. "I would never have done anything to hurt this baby. That pregnancy was my only chance to have a child of my own."

"Which is exactly why you shouldn't have pushed yourself so hard. You've been stressed out for months about finding your sister, not to mention the additional stress caused by renovations on the house and gallery. And why on earth you were teaching that art class in the first place is beyond me."

"I was trying to make a difference in those children's lives," she said in a quavering voice. "You were with me at my last checkup when they did the ultrasound. There were no signs the pregnancy was in trouble. You heard the doctor say that everything appeared to be perfectly normal and for me to go about my business as usual."

"You need to get your priorities straight, Ellie. The twins come first. We can't commit to another temporary situation with another child until we figure out this mess with your sister."

When he turned away from her, she grabbed him by the arm. "Please don't walk away from me. Listen, Dad will be here soon. Let's relax over dinner and a glass of wine, and then discuss this in a civilized manner after he leaves."

Julian yanked his arm free. "Go ahead and eat without me. I have work to do." He stomped off to his study, the sound of the door banging shut echoed throughout the hallway with a tone of finality.

Squeals of happiness drifted down from the upstairs hall bathroom. The twins would be out of the bath soon, and her father would arrive any minute. She stared down at her bathrobe. She would make herself presentable even if her heart wasn't in it. She would take Maddie's advice.

When you feel like it, you eat some food. When you have your strength back, whether that's today or the next day or next week, you put on some clothes, brush your hair, and face the world. Baby steps. She would start by facing her father. *Your heart is full of love, Miss Ellie Pringle Hagood. And there are plenty of people who need that love.*

The twins weren't the only ones who needed her love. She would stand her ground with Julian. She would not turn her back on Ruby, not when she had the means to provide her a safe and loving home.

She hurried upstairs to her room and changed into a pair of Bermuda shorts and a pale pink polo shirt. The woman staring back at her from the mirror had aged ten years in twenty-four hours. The dark circles under her eyes stood out like purple bruises against her pale complexion. But it was her eyes, red-rimmed and haunted, that gave her pause.

Ain't nothing gonna take away the pain but time, she reminded herself.

Her father had already arrived when she returned to the kitchen. He was sitting at the table with the girls, who were dressed in their pajamas, their dark manes still wet from their bath.

"What's all this?" Ellie asked, eyeing the colorful sheets of thick paper spread out on the table in front of the twins.

"GoPa brought us mack-neck-tick paper dolls!" Bella answered, stumbling on her words.

"Magnetic," Abbott corrected her.

"That's what I said! Mack-neck-tick," Bella said in a sassy tone.

Upon closer inspection, Ellie saw that each twin had a cutout of a Barbie doll and several plastic-coated magnetic sheets containing colorful outfits and accessories for Barbie to wear. "Oh wow. I used to love playing with paper dolls." She wagged her finger at her father. "You've got to stop spoiling them like this."

Abbott topped a cracker with Maddie's herb cheese spread

and handed it to her. "It's a GoPa's responsibility to spoil his grandchildren. And his daughter. How're you feeling?"

"Like I got hit by a locomotive."

"Why don't I fix you a glass of wine?" He got up and pulled out a bottle of sauvignon blanc from the refrigerator. After uncorking the bottle, he poured two glasses and handed one to her. "Where's Julian?"

"In his study, working on his new project. Don't count on him joining us for dinner," she said, bringing the glass to her lips. After her three months of abstinence, the wine tasted crisp and sweet.

Abbott knitted his brows together in concern. "Uh-oh. Something's wrong. Other than the obvious, of course. Want to talk about it?"

She shook her head. "Not really." But it was pointless to try to hide her feelings from her father.

He pulled one of the barstools out from beneath the counter. "Sit." She obeyed her father's command as though she were still a child. He sat down beside her. "Start talking."

"Remember I told you about Ruby, the little girl from my art class who I suspected was being abused?"

"I remember," he said with a nod.

"Well, her parents were arrested night before last." Ellie filled her father in on the details of the arrest and the events that had happened since. "Julian's against being her foster parent."

Abbott fed himself two more crackers and washed them down with wine. "You may not want to hear this, honey, but I need to be honest with you. I can't say I blame Julian for being upset. You should've talked to him about it before you went to the Department of Social Services."

"I realize I should've taken more time to think it through. But Julian and I have always seen eye to eye on everything. He's always supported me. I assumed he would this time as well. Maybe I don't know him as well as I thought I did. Maybe we should've taken more time to get to know each other before rushing into a marriage."

"If ever there were two people meant to be together, it's you and Julian. You just need to be patient, give him a chance to warm up to the idea. One of the things Julian loves the most about you is your passion for helping others." Abbott lowered his voice to nearly a whisper. "You just lost your baby, sweetheart. We all grieve in different ways. Some seek therapy while others suffer in silence. Give him some space. He'll feel better in a day or so."

Ellie stared down at the counter, the bowl of cheese spread blurred by her tears. "He has a lot going on right now with this new project. And I know he's worried about Katie," she said, and then explained her stepdaughter's recent odd behavior.

"Sounds like your husband has reason to be concerned." Abbott looked over at the twins, who were quietly playing with their paper dolls. "This unfinished business with Lia and the twins only complicates your lives more."

Ellie couldn't hold back any longer. The dam she'd held in place all afternoon broke and a torrent of tears flowed out.

Abbott reached for the paper towel roll and tore off a sheet. "I'm sorry, sweetheart," he said, handing it to her. "It was callous of me to mention Lia when you're already under enough pressure."

"It's true, though!" Ellie sobbed.

"You'll work it out in due time." Abbott massaged her back while she cried. "Until then, you lean on me for support. Tell me what I can do to help."

Ellie dabbed at her eyes with the paper towel. "I hate to ask you this when you've already done so much, but can you stay over again tonight? I don't trust myself with the twins, and I can't count on Julian right now. If one of them got sick during the night . . ."

"Say no more. I'd planned to stay anyway." He pushed back

from the bar and stood up. "I don't think this is helping any." He took her glass of wine from her and poured it down the drain. "Let's get you fed and off to bed. You need rest more than anything right now."

By the time they'd finished eating Maddie's fried chicken dinner, the twins were rubbing their tired eyes. "It's time for these beauties to go to bed," Abbott said, scooping one girl up in each arm.

Ellie moved to clear the table, and he said, "Leave those. I'll do them later."

But Ellie did the dishes anyway. She felt guilty for relying on her father as much as she had in recent days. Overwhelmed by events of the last few days and all the uncertainties looming in front of her, Ellie trudged up the stairs to her room. She crawled into bed fully clothed and cried into her pillow until she finally fell asleep some hours later.

She woke with a start shortly before three in the morning. Julian's side of the bed was empty, but she heard jazz music, the kind he listened to while he worked, coming from a distant part of the house. She smiled to herself. He was fortunate to have the Campbell project to take his mind off their problems.

Maybe she needed a project as well. Tomorrow, she would start a new painting.

POURING rain ruled out the possibility for outdoor activities on Saturday. *Just as well,* Ellie thought. The weather matched her mood. When her father left around ten to go home and work on his photography series, Ellie assured him that she and the twins would be fine.

"We're gonna watch Disney movies all day and eat all this yummy food Maddie left for us."

"Yay!" the girls responded, bouncing up and down on their toes.

They pushed the sofa and chairs out of the way and set up a camp with blankets and pillows on the floor of her studio. The girls played with their paper dolls, colored, and watched movies while Ellie stared at her stack of blank canvases across the room. She'd been contemplating several scenes in her neighborhood. She was tempted by a row of single houses with colorful doors and flowers flowing from window boxes on a street several blocks away. But another subject inspired her more. Her experience with portraiture was limited to what she'd learned in art school. But she felt compelled to paint the twins—to have something to remember them by when her sister came to reclaim them. She pulled out her sketchpad and began to draw.

Julian remained holed up in his study until three that afternoon. After a quick shower, he left the house without a word to Ellie or the girls. He'd still not returned when she retired for the night around nine. She tossed and turned, worried about where he might be. She ruled out the possibility that he'd gone to one of the many downtown bars. Julian was not one to drown his sorrows. At least from what she knew about him, which was turning out to be less than she thought. The Campbell property, currently empty of its occupants, was the only place that made sense.

Julian returned sometime during the night. His study door was once again closed the following morning. Desperate for a diversion, Ellie took the girls to Fuel for Sunday brunch and then for a walk along the seawall. When they arrived home at three, Julian was gone again. The doorbell rang as she was tucking the twins in for their nap, and Ellie was shocked to see Julian's daughter on her piazza, her purple suitcase on the wooden floor at her feet. Her chin quivered, and her eyes were puffy and red-rimmed from crying.

"Katie!" Ellie embraced the trembling child. "What on earth are you doing here, honey?"

"I ran away from home!" she cried.

Ellie held the child at arm's length. "You mean your mother doesn't know where you are?"

Katie shook her head. "We got in a fight last night. I told her I was gonna run away, and she told me not to come back."

Ellie fought to keep a straight face despite her alarm.

Who would say such a thing to an eight-year-old child?

"How did you get here?"

"I used Mom's phone to order an Uber to take me to the bus station."

"How did you leave the house without your mother seeing you?"

"She was passed out, drunk. She didn't have any money in her wallet. I had to spend my savings on the bus ticket. Can you please pay the taxi driver who brought me here from the station?"

Ellie straightened. She hadn't noticed the yellow taxi waiting at the curb. "Of course. Let me get my wallet." She held a finger up to the driver, signaling she'd be with him in a minute. Retrieving her purse from the console table, she paid the driver the fare plus a hefty tip for taking such good care of the little girl. She turned her back on the taxi as it drove away from the curb.

"Let's get you inside," she said, kissing the top of Katie's honey-colored head. "You've come a long way all by your lonesome. Are you hungry?"

Katie's slate-blue eyes blinked back tears. "I'm starving. Do you have any pimento cheese?"

Ellie laughed. "As a matter of fact, I do." She dropped Katie's suitcase at the bottom of the stairs, and they walked hand in hand down the hall. "Wait until you see the kitchen. They finally finished the renovations."

Katie circled the kitchen before sliding onto a barstool to await her sandwich. Ellie spread pimento cheese on wheat bread and poured a glass of milk. She set both on the counter in front of her stepdaughter. "Do you think your mother has any idea where you are?"

The child lifted a bony shoulder. "I didn't tell her, but she probably knows."

Ellie checked her landline and her cell phone for any missed calls from Katie's mother. But there were none. If Laura had called Julian to alert him their daughter was missing, he would've rushed home in a panic to wait for her.

"Your father's not here right now. He's working on a new project. But I imagine he'll be back soon." Ellie poured herself a glass of sweet tea and sat next to Katie. "Do you wanna tell me why you ran away?"

"I don't want to live in Spartanburg anymore," Katie said, pinching off a bite of her sandwich. "Can I live here in Charleston with you and Daddy?"

"It's not that simple," Ellie said. "In order for that to happen, your father would need to get permission from the judge, who will want to know what's going on at home that's made you so unhappy."

"I hate Mommy," Katie said, pushing her plate away. "She's mean, and I don't have any friends."

"What about your friends on your soccer team?"

"They're not *my* friends." She jabbed a thumb at her chest. "The other moms on the team are Mommy's friends. She picked the team for me."

"I thought you loved soccer."

"I do! I just don't like this team. We travel every weekend. The moms go out to bars at night and leave the kids to run around the hotel. The other girls do bad things. They play pranks on the other people staying at the hotel. I usually just stay in my room." Katie took a sip of milk and licked her lips. "On the weekends when we don't have soccer tournaments, she makes up excuses for me to miss my visitations with Daddy. She told me he doesn't love me anymore, that his new family is more important to him. Is that true, Ellie?"

Ellie's eyes grew huge. "That is absolutely not true." She tilted the little girl's chin toward her. "You listen to me. Your father loves you more than anything in the world. And I adore you. You are welcome here anytime. Not seeing you these past few months has made your daddy very sad."

Katie's face broke into a big smile. "Really?"

"Really!" Ellie reached for her cell phone. "But I need to call your father and let him know you're here." She dialed Julian's number. The line rang twice before going to voice mail.

She typed out a text: *Have you heard from Laura today? Katie ran away from home. She took the bus to Charleston. She's here with me safe and sound.*

Her phone immediately pinged with an incoming text from him: *Almost home.*

A minute later, the back door opened and Julian entered the room. He pulled his daughter off her barstool and hugged her tight. "Are you all right?"

"I'm fine, now that I'm here with you," she said, her small arms squeezing his neck.

He danced her over to the table and sat down on the banquette bench with Katie on his lap. "Tell me what happened."

Ellie stood at the island, listening as Katie repeated her story. The more his daughter talked, the darker his face grew.

"Can I live here with you, Daddy?" Katie asked when she finished.

He kissed the side of her face at her temple. "I'm going to do everything in my power to make that happen. But you might have to go back to Spartanburg to finish the school year. It won't be too bad. You only have a few weeks left."

"Please don't make me go back," Katie said, burying her face in his chest.

"I could homeschool her," Ellie offered. "If her teacher is

willing to work with us. Becca will help. Together, we can figure out third-grade math."

Julian's face was filled with gratitude as he mouthed "Thank you" to Ellie. He drew his daughter away from him so he could look her in the eyes. "I need to make a few phone calls, to see what I can find out."

Ellie held her hand out to Katie. "While he does that, why don't you and I take your suitcase up to your room? You can wake the twins up from their nap. They'll be so excited to see you."

ELLIE

*J*ulian spoke with his ex-wife on his cell phone for over an hour. Standing outside his study, Ellie listened through the door, but she couldn't make out a word of what he said despite his raised and angry tone. He didn't mention the conversation during dinner except to tell Katie he planned to call the principal of her school first thing the following morning.

Much to Ellie's relief, his anger toward her had metamorphosed into concern for his daughter. Witnessing his love for his only child caused Ellie's heart to break all over again, knowing he would never experience that same kind of love for their baby.

Julian spent the morning in his study, on the phone, working out the logistics so Katie could finish her school year from Charleston. When he mysteriously disappeared for most of the afternoon, she assumed he was down the street working on the Campbell project. Ellie and Katie spread her books out on the dining room table, and subject by subject, they made a list of the projects that needed completing before the end of the year.

Ellie was grateful to see her husband in a pleasant mood at dinner. With a twinkle in his eye that she hadn't seen for days, he announced that he and Katie would go to Spartanburg the next day to pick up more of her belongings and meet with her teachers about her schoolwork for the remainder of the year.

Ellie was standing at the end of the sidewalk on Tuesday morning, waving Julian and Katie off, when Franny's station wagon pulled up to the curb. Ruby hopped out and ran into Ellie's open arms. She planted kisses in the girl's frizzy orange hair. She felt a unique bond with this child. Ellie knew all too well what it was like to be a child all alone in the world, with no one to love her.

Franny retrieved Ruby's suitcase from the back of her wagon and approached them. "We're here to support you, Ellie. Do not hesitate to reach out to me or anyone on my staff for whatever you need."

"I don't understand," Ellie said, flabbergasted. "This is amazing. But how did this happen without Julian's paperwork?"

"Didn't he tell you? He came to our office yesterday and personally handed in his paperwork. He convinced Beth to expedite the process. Your husband can be quite persuasive. He had the connections to make this miracle happen."

Her heart swelled with love for her husband. He hadn't mentioned a word. He'd succeeded in surprising her with the biggest gift he could've given her.

Ellie smiled. "That sounds like Julian."

"Now," Franny said. "Since you reside in the same school district, Ruby will continue at Peninsula Elementary. She missed most of last week. It's best if she can return to school as soon as she gets settled."

Ruby tilted her head up to Ellie. "Can I go today?"

Ellie brushed an orange curl off her forehead. "Of course you can. Have you eaten breakfast yet?"

"No, ma'am. I didn't feel much like eating at the home."

"Then you must be starving." Ellie took Ruby's suitcase from

Franny. "Let's go inside and see what Maddie has on her breakfast menu. After you eat, I'll take you to school."

They bid Franny goodbye and turned toward the house.

"Whoa." Ruby's mouth formed an O as she stared up at the house. "How many people live here?"

Ellie paused at the front door. "Hmm. There's my husband and me. My three-year-old twin nieces. My stepdaughter, Katie. And now you. Six people total—two big and four little."

She opened the door and stepped aside for Ruby to enter. Leaving Ruby's suitcase in the hallway, she led the child to the back of the house. Maddie looked up from her griddle and the twins from their coloring when Ellie entered the kitchen with Ruby.

"Mya, Bella, Maddie, I'd like you to meet a special friend of mine. This is Ruby. She's going to be living with us for a while."

"Did your mommy go away, too?" Bella asked, her chocolate eyes full of concern.

Ruby cast an uncertain glance at Ellie.

"Yes, sweetheart," Ellie answered for her. "Ruby's mother had to go away, just like yours."

Maddie waved her spatula at the pancakes on the griddle. "Do you like flapjacks, Ruby?"

"Yes, ma'am," Ruby said, smacking her lips as she eyed the pancakes.

Maddie cackled. "Good! I love a child with an appetite."

Scrambling off the bench, Bella and Mya nearly tripped over each other as they hurried over to inspect the newcomer. "Why is your hair that color?" Mya asked.

Ruby smiled. "The same reason yours is brown."

"Why do you have spots all over your face and arms?" Bella wanted to know.

"Those are freckles," Ruby said, rubbing her arm. "My mama says my freckles mark the spots where angels kissed me when I was born."

"Come color with us," Bella said, taking Ruby by the hand and pulling her over to the table.

Maddie flipped the pancakes with her spatula. "You're doing a good thing, Miss Ellie. It's a crying shame the way some mamas abuse and neglect their chil'run. I don't know what's become of folks these days."

Ellie was struck by the irony that she had in her care four children abandoned and mistreated by their mothers when she was unable to have a baby of her own. "We're a family of misfits, Maddie."

"Maybe so, Miss Ellie. But there's a lot of love in your house of misfits."

Ellie went to the refrigerator and poured three glasses of orange juice for the girls.

"Having additional people living in the house will create more work for you. I'm thinking of hiring someone to do the heavy cleaning, to lighten your workload so you can spend more time in the kitchen, but I wanted to discuss it with you first."

"I'm all for it," Maddie said. "These old bones of mine been acting up lately."

"Do you know anyone who might be looking for a job?"

"I may know of someone." Maddie transferred stacks of pancakes onto three plates and added several slices of bacon to each. "I know a real sweet girl, honest and hardworking, who's looking for work. Want me to bring her round one afternoon this week?"

"Please! The sooner the better, with the twins' birthday party next Sunday," Ellie said as she delivered the plates to the table.

"Is Ruby coming to our party?" Mya asked.

"Of course she is." Ellie sat down at the table with her coffee. "The twins are turning four on Thursday," she explained to Ruby. "We're having a party next Sunday to celebrate. My husband has invited the whole neighborhood. There will be children of all ages here, so you can make some new friends."

"I've never been to a birthday party before." Ruby stuffed the whole slice of bacon in her mouth at once. "Will there be cake?" she asked with her mouth full.

Ellie bit her lip to keep from laughing. "Of course! A party isn't a party without cake. What kind of cake are we having, Maddie?"

The housekeeper planted her hands on her hips. "You can ask me that all day long, but I ain't gonna tell you. It's a surprise. You'll just have to wait and see."

"Aunt Ellie! Look what Ruby drew," Bella said, waving a piece of computer paper in the air.

Ellie took the paper from her and studied the drawing of a sailboat on the harbor. The child appeared to have more talent than she'd originally suspected. "This is really good, Ruby. You did a nice job of shading to give the appearance of the sun reflecting off the water."

Ruby smiled bashfully. "Blue's my favorite color."

Ellie archived that information for later, when she planned to go shopping for Ruby's room. "I can tell. I love the way you incorporated different shades of blue—teal and cobalt and a hint of periwinkle."

Ruby shoveled in a forkful of pancakes. "I missed a lot of school, Mrs. Hagood. Do you think I can finish my self-portrait today?"

"Since you'll be living with us, Ruby, I'd like it if you'd call me Ellie. Or Miss Ellie. Whichever you feel more comfortable with." She sipped her coffee. "As for your self-portrait, I'm sad to say I'm no longer teaching your art class."

Ruby stuck her lower lip out in a pout.

"Tell you what," Ellie said. "Why don't we bring your project home and finish it here?"

Ruby grinned. "I'd like that, Miss Ellie."

"And I like hearing you call me Miss Ellie." She took a sip of coffee. "You know what? I have a large studio over my art gallery downtown. Maybe we can schedule some workshops for your classmates over the summer."

"Really?" Ruby dropped her fork on her plate with a loud clamor. "Do you mean it? That would be so much fun."

"Sure, I mean it." Ellie was warming up to the idea. She couldn't wait to see the look on Rose Bellamy's face when she found out Ellie was providing art lessons for free to her students. "In that case, why don't you ask them what days would work best for them? Can I count on you to help me organize the workshops?"

"Yes!" Ruby said, rising up out of her seat a little. "Anything you need."

The sadness that had taken up residence in Ellie's chest the past few days subsided just a little. She had parties to plan, art classes to organize, and bedrooms to decorate. She couldn't possibly love these four little girls more if they were her own biological children. For however long they lived with her, she would do everything in her power to protect and provide for them.

ELLIE

*E*llie spent much of the day on Tuesday shopping for and sprucing up Ruby's room. Hers was the smallest of the five bedrooms upstairs, but Ellie thought it the most charming of all, tucked away in the back corner of the house with an abundance of natural light streaming in through two windows. Everything in the room was white—walls, lattice headboard, matching nightstands—which provided a clean canvas for the vibrant hues of greens and blues in the geometric shapes on the quilt, aqua shaggy rug, and pair of sea glass table lamps Ellie purchased on her shopping spree.

She had everything in place by the time she went to pick Ruby up from school that afternoon.

"The colors are like the Caribbean Ocean," Ruby said with delight when she saw the room. "I've never been to the islands, but I've seen pictures on TV and always wanted to go."

"I'm glad you like it," Ellie said. She left her new foster child to unpack her meager belongings in the white lacquer chest of drawers.

In spite of Fanny's revelation that Julian had submitted his portion of the foster parent application, Ellie feared his response to Ruby's sudden appearance in their home. But when they arrived from Spartanburg around six that evening, it was Katie's reaction, not Julian's, that surprised her.

Ellie was helping Julian and Katie unload the odd assortment of duffel bags and plastic bins packed with clothes and other personal belongings from the car when Katie noticed Ruby sitting at Ellie's desk in her studio. "Who is that girl, and what's she doing here?"

"That's Ruby," Ellie said. "She's one of my art students, and she's going to be living here with us for a while. I'm her foster mother."

"Does that make you her foster father?" Katie asked Julian, who had entered the hallway behind her with an armful of hanging clothes.

"Yes, sweetheart, I will be her foster parent. And I'm looking forward to meeting my new foster daughter." Julian dropped the hanging clothes in a heap at the foot of the stairs. "Ruby's had a difficult time lately. Ellie and I are fortunate to be in a position to offer her a safe place to live, and we're happy to have her here."

"That's just great! I finally get to live with my daddy again and I have to share him with all these other children," Katie said, and stomped off to her room.

"Dinner's in thirty minutes," Ellie called after her. She turned to her husband. "Thank you for what you did, Julian. For pulling whatever strings you pulled to make this happen."

"It was worth it to see the smile return to your face. Anyway, the more children the merrier, in my opinion." He smiled at Ellie with the love and kindness she hadn't felt from him in weeks.

"Our house of misfits," she said in a soft voice. "I hope Katie will adjust."

He took Ellie in his arms. "She'll be fine. She needs to learn how to share. Her mother has spoiled her. Laura has let her do whatever she wants, at least in most things—obviously not in letting her choose her own soccer team or honoring her weekend visitations with me. I get the impression that it's easier for Laura to give in than say no."

She relaxed against him, comforted by the feel of his body close to hers. "Judging from the amount of stuff y'all brought from Spartanburg, she's giving you full custody."

He planted kisses in the crook of her neck. "At least for the summer. I'm not sure what's going on with Laura. She's changed, and not for the better."

"For Katie's sake, I'm sorry to hear that."

"Katie is fortunate to have a wonderful stepmother in you." Julian held her at arm's length. "I owe you an apology. It's been a difficult couple of weeks, and I haven't made it any easier for you. But I want you to know I'm sorry for that and I love you very much."

"And I love you. I've made my share of mistakes as well. I don't like it when we fight. Can we make a pact to work together going forward?"

He offered his hand, and they shook on it. "We'll have to do something about your car. You can't fit all of these children in that Matchbox of yours."

Ellie burst out laughing. "What'd you have in mind?"

"A sporty SUV of some sort. One that has a third row of seats. I know a dealer who will work us a sweet price," he said, his eyes full of mischief.

She play-slapped him. "I'm sure you do."

"We have a lot to talk about. Let's feed our brood so we can have some time to ourselves." Taking her by the hand, he led her to the kitchen. "What're we having for dinner?"

"Maddie left a lasagna in the oven. Why don't you set the table while I toss the salad?"

Julian greeted Ruby with kindness when Ellie introduced them. Ruby blushed crimson, and then warmed right up to him as they worked together to put the plates, silverware, and napkins on the table. But when Katie joined them and they gathered around the table for the first time as a family, the air was thick with tension. After Julian offered the blessing, the twins babbled on about their upcoming party while everyone else ate in silence. Katie stared openly at Ruby when she scooped up her beans with her spoon. Ellie had noticed the girl's table manners were lacking, but decided not to embarrass her by mentioning it tonight. She could work on it with Ruby after things settled down.

"So . . . I mentioned it to Ellie, and she agrees that what this family needs is a week at the beach," Julian said as he slathered butter on a slice of Italian bread.

Katie's head shot up. "Can we really, Daddy? Please, oh please. We can rent our same house on Sullivan's Island."

Ellie's heart sank. She loved the idea of spending a week at the beach with her new family, just not in the same beach house where he'd vacationed every year with his ex-wife and their child.

"Not the same house, sweetheart," he said. "I've found a house I think you'll love just as much if not better. It's right on the ocean and big enough for all of us to have our own rooms, even Becca if she's willing to come with us."

"Who's Becca?" Katie asked.

"Our babysitter," Bella piped in.

"For the summer," Ellie added. "She just graduated from the College of Charleston and is looking for a full-time job. She was on the sailing team. Maybe she can teach us to sail."

"Can GoPa come?" Mya asked.

"Of course he can. Maddie too, if she wants. The house has a gazillion bedrooms." Julian pinched off a piece of bread. "I've got a hold on the house for the second week in June. If everyone is in agreement, I'll secure the rental with a deposit."

Katie raised her hand. "I'm in!"

"Me too!" the twins chanted in unison.

"What about you, Ruby?" Ellie asked. "What do you think about spending a week at the beach?"

Ruby stared down at her plate. "I wasn't sure I was invited."

"We wouldn't go on a trip and not take you," Julian said. "You're part of the family now, Ruby."

"But I don't know how to swim," Ruby said in a small voice.

"We can remedy that easily enough with swimming lessons this summer," Julian said.

Ellie placed an arm around Ruby and gave her a little squeeze. "Knowing how to swim is not required for spending a week at the beach. We can paint and build sand castles and look for shells. How does that sound?"

A smile tugged at the corners of her mouth. "Good."

Ellie glanced across the table at Katie, who was studying Ruby with a softer set of eyes. For the rest of dinner, they talked about all the activities they would do and food they would eat while at the beach.

When everyone had finished eating, Julian pushed back from the table. "Today has been an exhausting one for all of us. I'll take the twins up for their bath while y'all do the dishes." He scooped one twin under each arm and carried them, giggling hysterically, out of the kitchen.

"We'll need to go shopping for our trip to the beach," Ellie said as she stacked the dirty plates and carried them to the sink.

Katie positioned herself at the sink and began rinsing dishes. "I could definitely use a new bathing suit."

Aha! Just the response I was hoping for, thought Ellie.

"Why don't we go tomorrow after Ruby gets home from school?" She elbow-bumped Katie as she handed her another stack of dishes. "We'll count on you to show us the good places to shop."

Katie's ponytail danced across her shoulders as she bobbed her head up and down. "I can do that. So, Ruby, are you a pants person or do you like dresses more?"

Ruby shrugged. "I never thought about it. I usually wear whatever my mother can afford to buy me from Goodwill."

Katie's mouth dropped open and her eyes narrowed, but she

recovered quickly. "Then we'll have to figure out what looks best when we go shopping tomorrow."

An hour later, as Ellie emerged from the twins' room after reading two bedtime stories, she noticed Ruby's door ajar and heard mumbled voices coming from within. She eavesdropped from the hallway.

"What happened to your parents?" Katie asked.

"My daddy's dead, and my mama's in prison," Ruby said.

"Prison? Wow!" Katie said, and Ellie imagined her stepdaughter's expression of astonishment.

"She can stay there forever, for all I care."

"I'm mad at my mom, too." Katie lowered her voice and said something she couldn't hear.

To respect their privacy, Ellie moved away from the door. She returned to the kitchen and finished straightening up. When she came back upstairs at nine thirty, all four of her girls were sound asleep.

She slipped between the cool sheets beside her husband. He set the mystery novel he was reading on the night table and turned toward her. He tossed his leg over her midsection and melded his body to hers. "I feel like the old man who lives in the shoe."

Ellie giggled. "Who had so many children he didn't know what to do?"

"Mm-hmm. Something like that." He dragged his finger across her forehead and down her nose to her lips. "How are you feeling? About the miscarriage, I mean. I'm not avoiding the subject on purpose. But so much has happened these past few days with Katie . . ."

"Shh!" Ellie pressed the tip of her finger against his lips. "I understand. We don't need to talk about it."

"Yes, we do. At least I do. I need to say this." He propped himself on one elbow. "I don't know what got into me. The

131

emotional side of me blamed you for losing the baby, even though the rational side of me knows it wasn't your fault."

"You had every right to blame me. God gave me a gift, a little life to protect and nurture, and I failed him. Which is why it's so important for me not to fail Ruby. Or the twins or Katie. He's counting on me. I can't let him down a second time."

"You won't, babe. I'll make certain you don't."

Ellie snuggled into him. "Tell me about Katie. What kind of deal did you work out with her mother?"

"Like I told you earlier, Laura has agreed to let Katie live with me for the summer. Laura doesn't know this, but I'm petitioning for full custody. Based on what Katie told me and what I witnessed with my own eyes today, I'm not sure she'll fight it. My ex-wife is going through some kind of premature midlife crisis. She was still in bed with a hangover when we arrived at eleven o'clock this morning. It's like she's reliving her college years all over again. If she's not careful, she'll get fired from her job."

"Do you have any idea what this is about?"

"I'm not sure. I'm starting to think she's having some emotional problems. She up and left me without any warning, and now this. She's no longer my problem except where my daughter is concerned." He lay his head against Ellie's breast. "I'm submitting an application for Katie to Ashley Hall, which is where she went for kindergarten. I'm sure they're already full for the fall term, but I know some of the board members."

"Sure you do," Ellie said, nudging him with her elbow. "I've been thinking about Ruby's education as well. She's so bright, and we have the means to provide her a good education. But if we have custody of her for only one year, would it be cruel to let her attend private school and then yank the opportunity away from her?"

"From what you've told me, I think her mother will be in jail for longer than a year. But one year of private school is better than no years, in my opinion. The teachers and students she will meet and the experiences she encounters could have a profound impact on the rest of her life. Why don't I put in an application for both girls?"

Ellie turned to him. "Would you do that for Ruby?"

"Of course, sweetheart. We will treat all our children equally as long as they live under our roof. I pray that's until they are ready to go to college and be out on their own."

LIA

*L*ia spent nine days in Daytona Beach—swimming and soaking up the rays by day, dancing and having uninhibited sex with strange men by night. Until now, she'd made love with only two men in her life—her husband and Justin. She'd been missing out on life's best-kept secret. Sex was better than any drug she'd ever tried, prescription or recreational, for satisfying her addictive personality.

The effects of the lithium had long since worn off, and she was feeling like her old self again. She was riding a high more exhilarating than she'd ever experienced before. The depths of darkness lurked beneath the surface of that high. But she wouldn't think about that now. She planned to enjoy herself while the good time lasted.

She was now a regular at Hank's Honky Tonk, where the music was twangy, the rednecks rugged, and the draft beer cheap. Not that she ever ordered more than one. The beer was a prop. How sexy would she look drinking lemonade while perched on a stool at the polished wooden bar?

The neon Budweiser sign hanging above the shelves of liquor bottles behind the bar brought to mind the image of her husband's dead body. The brilliant red of the bowtie in the logo was exactly the shade of the blood soaking the sheets of his hotel bed. Her eyes traveled the restaurant as she searched for signs of uniformed policemen. She didn't see any, but that didn't mean they weren't there. They'd been following her since she left Key West, hiding behind the sand dunes on the beach and peeking through the window of her motel room. It was entirely possible these figures were a figment of her imagination, that darkness lurking in the shadows.

The partiers flowed into Hank's beginning around ten o'clock. Most were strangers, but Lia recognized a few familiar faces, even one particularly hot guy she'd banged two nights ago in the back seat of his pickup truck in Hank's parking lot.

What was his name? James? No. That wasn't it. Noah. Noah from Nebraska.

Someone dropped coins in the jukebox and selected David Lee Murphy's "Party Crowd." The room erupted into cheers, and couples flowed out onto the dance floor. A good-looking cowboy in boots and blue jeans, with a body that rocked his Kyle Busch T-shirt, slipped onto the empty barstool beside her.

"Evening, gorgeous. What say I buy you a tequila shot and we get naked together?"

She awarded him her brightest smile. "Why waste time with tequila?"

"Ooh, baby." He slid off his barstool, pulled her to her feet, and two-stepped her out onto the dance floor. Pulling her to him, he buried his face in the silk scarf around her neck. They danced together, tangled in each other's arms. By the fifth song, they were making out hot and heavy, oblivious to onlookers.

A tiny blonde-haired woman whose head was too big for her body tapped Lia's dance partner on the shoulder. "Are you kidding me right now, Brad? I turn my back on you for an hour, and you jump into the arms of the first slut who looks your way."

Lia turned away from Brad and faced the woman. "Who are you?"

"I'm his wife." The petite woman shoved Lia away, and with fists clenched at her side, she stared her husband down. "You ditched me at our hotel, and I find you here dancing with this little tramp. What's up with that, Brad?"

Brad cocked his head to the side. "Aw, come on, Mel. I'm just having a little fun, like that time last year I caught you making out with Jake the Snake at our block party. Go on back to the room now. I won't be out too late."

Mel crossed her arms over her chest, refusing to budge.

"You heard the man," Lia said. "Beat it."

"Why, you little slut." Mel took a swing at Lia, but Lia ducked before her fist crashed into her face.

She grabbed Mel's arm, twisting it behind her back, and brought her lips close to Mel's ear. "You can have him. He sucks in bed anyway."

Of course it was a lie. She'd never met Brad before that night. But feeling Mel squirm in anger was worth it.

Turning the woman loose, Lia spun on her heels and sauntered out of Hank's Honky Tonk. She'd grown bored of Daytona. It was time to move on. First thing tomorrow morning, she would board a bus for South Carolina.

*E*llie gave Katie her choice of restaurants when they decided to go for a late lunch the following day. Leon's is famous for their Southern-style soul food, but instead of ordering the fried chicken platter, Katie surprised Ellie by asking for a dozen raw oysters.

"You're a girl after her father's heart," Ellie said when the waitress had finished taking their order. "He does love his seafood raw."

Katie smiled. "Believe it or not, I was still in diapers when Daddy fed me my first oyster." Her blue eyes were bright with hope when she leaned across the table toward Ellie. "Do you think I'll get to live here permanently with y'all?"

"If your father has his way about it, you will. And I would certainly love to have you. And the twins and Ruby. You make our odd little family feel complete."

"I'm used to being an only child, but I kinda like having other kids around." She dropped her smile and scrunched her face up. "I'll run away again if my mom tries to make me go back to Spartanburg. She doesn't care about me anymore. All she cares about are her friends."

"Now, Katie, you know that's not true. Your mom loves you." The waitress arrived with their sweet teas. Ellie waited for her to leave again before she asked, "These friends you mentioned—are they the soccer moms you told me about the other day?"

Katie nodded as she slurped tea through her straw. "When we moved to Spartanburg, instead of working in a neonatal unit at a hospital like when we lived here, Mom got a job in a pediatrician's office so she could be home with me at night. I don't know why she bothered. She goes out almost every night and leaves me at home alone."

Why would Laura leave her eight-year-old daughter home alone at night?

Ellie reminded herself that children Katie's age were prone to exaggeration. "When you say she goes out, what exactly do you mean?"

"I mean she goes out with her friends to bars and stays out until past midnight. She used to get up every morning and fix breakfast for me before school, but she doesn't even do that anymore."

The server delivered Katie's platter of raw oysters and a grilled mahi sandwich for Ellie and quickly scurried off to assist another table.

Ellie lifted the bun on her sandwich and examined her fish. "What time does your mother have to be at work?"

"At nine." Katie dipped an oyster in cocktail sauce and popped it in her mouth. "She's usually still in bed when I leave for the bus stop at seven thirty. I don't know how she makes it to work on time, but I guess she does. I mean, they haven't fired her or anything yet."

Katie had matured quite a lot since Christmas. Having to fend for oneself made a little girl grow up too soon. "I'm sorry, sweetheart. I know this has been a difficult time for you. But you can relax now, and let the grown-ups take care of you."

While they ate, Katie offered more details about life with her mother in Spartanburg. By the time she'd finished paying the check, Ellie was angry with the child's mother, but she tried not to let her irritation show. She made mental notes to share with Julian instead.

They left Leon's and went straight to Peninsula Elementary to pick up Ruby. From there, they drove to the Tanger Outlets in North Charleston.

Katie and Ruby, their arms loaded with clothes on hangers, disappeared into the same dressing room at the Gap. Even though a year separated the girls in age, Katie, who had inherited her father's height, wore the same size as Ruby. They shopped at Old Navy, the Children's Place, and J.Crew. They purchased two new dresses and a bathing suit for Katie, and a whole new wardrobe for Ruby. Ellie's heart swelled with happiness to see the girls giggling and whispering and carrying on like best friends. As they left the mall, she treated them to ice cream cones despite the close proximity to the dinner hour.

When they arrived home, Ellie carried a load of shopping bags upstairs and deposited them on Ruby's bed. She heard shrieks of laughter coming from the twins' playroom and crossed the hall to check on them. Becca was stretched out on the daybed, texting on her phone, while Bella and Mya danced plastic horses across the floor at her feet.

Ellie dropped to her knees beside them. "Whatcha got there?"

"GoPa bought us Buy-her horses." Bella handed Ellie a horse with reddish coloring. "See, Aunt Ellie! This one looks like you."

She took the horse from Bella. "I believe they're called Breyer Horses."

Mya pranced a buckskin horse with black tail and mane across the floor toward Ellie. "And this one looks like Mommy. We saw her today."

Ellie's heart skipped a beat, but her face remained impassive. "You saw who today?"

"Mommy." Bella crawled into Ellie's lap and wrapped her

arms around her neck. "Do we have to go home with her, Aunt Ellie? We really like it here with you and Julian."

"No, sweetheart, you're staying right here with us." Ellie cuddled the child. "Are you sure it was your mommy?"

Mya nodded. "She talked to us."

Ellie swallowed the lump in her throat. "Where did you see her?"

"In the park," Mya said.

"Where was Becca when this happened?" Ellie shot a glance at the sitter, whose color had drained from her face.

"Talking on her cell phone," Mya mumbled, chewing on her lower lip.

Becca was saved from having to respond by the sound of the front door closing and footsteps in the downstairs hall.

When Julian called out, "Fam, I'm home," Bella and Mya scrambled to their feet and raced each other out of the room.

Ellie and Becca stood to face each other. "I'm so sorry, Mrs. Hagood. I was only on the phone with my mom for a minute. She had a breast biopsy today, and I was worried about her," Becca said with a quaver in her voice.

Ellie's anger subsided a little. "I'm sorry to hear about your mom. I hope everything's all right."

"Yes, ma'am. They don't think it's cancer."

"That's good news. I know you're relieved. But we still need to talk about what happened in the park today. You realize it only takes a minute to kidnap a child."

Becca hung her blonde head. "Yes, ma'am. I saw a skinny woman with dark hair talking to them. She let them pet her little dog. I had no idea it was their mother."

Dog? Ellie thought. *Lia doesn't seem like the pet-loving type.*

"No harm done this time." She squeezed Becca's bicep. "I'm partially to blame anyway. I should have told you about their mother sooner." She removed her cell phone from her jacket pocket and showed Bella the picture of her sister. "Was this the woman you saw talking to them?"

Becca studied the photograph. "I can't say for sure. The woman in the park was wearing a baseball cap pulled low over her face."

Ellie slipped the phone back in her pocket. "I've neither seen nor heard from Lia in the seven months since she left the twins in my care. I don't even know that much about her. We were raised by different parents. But I'm concerned she may have mental problems. Let's keep the twins close to home for the next few days until we find out what my sister is up to."

Becca offered her a sympathetic smile. "Yes, ma'am. I understand."

Ellie glanced at her watch. "I realize it's time for you to leave, but can you stay a few minutes longer while I explain the situation to Julian?"

"I'm happy to stay as long as you need me," Becca said, and they walked out of the room and down the stairs together.

ELLIE SUMMONED Julian to his study, and they called her father on the speakerphone. "We have a situation," she said. "Lia has come back to Charleston to claim the twins. She approached them in the park today."

"Where was Becca?" Abbott asked.

"Talking to her mother on her cell phone. Her mother had a breast biopsy today. Naturally, she was concerned about her. I've never explained the situation to Becca, so she didn't know to be on the lookout for Lia."

"That makes no sense, Ellie. Why have you never told your babysitter that her charges' mother could be dangerous?"

Ellie winced at her father's accusatory tone. "I don't know,

Dad. I was worried about scaring her off, I guess. I realize now it was a mistake not to tell her."

"No sense beating yourself up about it now, as long as Becca understands the severity of the situation. Should we call the police?"

"Why would we call the police?" Ellie asked.

Julian's eyes met hers. "Because your sister is wanted for questioning in a murder investigation."

Ellie considered this for thirty seconds before responding. "That's true, and we have the safety of others to consider now that Katie and Ruby are in the picture. Actually, we don't even know for certain it was Lia in the park. I would think the twins would know their own mother. Then again, they're so young, and it's been seven months since they last saw her. On the other hand, if it *was* Lia, and if we make her angry, she could take the twins, and we may never see them again."

"Agreed on all points," Julian said. "Why don't we let Lia make the next move? In the meantime, we'll consult with our attorney. He understands the situation. He can advise us on how to proceed."

"I guess that's reasonable," Abbot said with an audible sigh. "But it wouldn't hurt to be extra cautious. I can make myself available to sit with the twins. I know you have your hands full with Katie and Ruby."

"You're welcome here anytime, Dad. You know that. I'm interviewing a young woman tomorrow, a friend of Maddie's, to take over the heavy cleaning. With four children, two adults, and two dogs, Maddie—God bless her—is too old to maintain this household without help. If I like Cilla, I plan to hire her on the spot, which will free up some of Maddie's time to help keep an eye on the twins."

"Good," Abbott said. "We'll have plenty of people in place to be on the lookout for trouble."

LIA

*T*he last of Lia's money bought her six nights in a cheap hotel room in a sketchy part of downtown Charleston. The desk clerk insisted she pay in advance. She hoped that would give her enough time to take care of business. She'd never had much of an appetite for food, but when the hunger got the best of her, she was forced to forage for leftovers. Charleston hosted some of the best restaurants in the Southeast. In the back alleys behind those restaurants were dumpsters that housed the spoils from their tables.

Charleston was a walking city, and pacing the streets of downtown calmed her restless soul. Temporarily, anyway. Her anticipation was mounting. She wouldn't be able to control her excitement much longer.

She spied on her sister from behind trees in the park across from her house and crouched between cars parked along the street she lived on. She peeped though the iron gate at the twins playing in the garden and hid in the foundation shrubs, listening to their squeals of laughter through the open kitchen window. Lia was certain that, as she'd intended, Bella and Mya had reported their encounter in the park to Ellie. She thought it priceless the way her sister looked over her shoulder on her way to her car and darted quick glances up and down the street when she went out for the newspaper. Resisting the temptation to jump out of her hiding place and yell, "Boo!" Lia forced herself to wait for the right opportunity instead. And that opportunity presented itself on Thursday evening. She stood by the garden gate eavesdropping on Ellie and Julian, who were, as best she could tell from the sound of their voices, seated at the umbrellaed table on the terrace. Lia propped herself against the brick wall, casually crossing her feet to give the impression to late-afternoon strollers that she was waiting for a friend.

Her sister's sugary sweet voice drifted toward her. "The twins would be so disappointed if we canceled the party."

Lia's ears perked up. *Party?*

"I think we're probably in the clear," Julian said. "If Lia is the woman the twins saw in the park on Wednesday, I feel certain she would've made herself known by now."

"I'm sure you're right," Ellie said. "The woman with the dog probably resembled Lia, and the twins' wishful thinking convinced them it was their mother. Just in case, we'll have plenty of help here on Sunday to be on the lookout for her."

Sunday! The party's on Sunday.

"I've asked Maddie and Cilla to help. Of course, Dad will be here and he's bringing Lacey."

Who's Cilla?

"Hiring Cilla was a good move," Julian said. "She's a hard worker and pleasant to have around."

Another maid. I'm not surprised. Wouldn't want Ellie Darling changing bed linens or cleaning toilets.

Ellie's voice again. "I think Maddie is secretly relieved to have some help. The housework was getting too much for her."

Maddie, that old cow. She should've retired years ago.

"After most of the guests arrive, we'll station Dad and Lacey at the front door, Becca at the activities stations, and Cilla in the kitchen, which will leave Maddie free to help out wherever she's needed."

Bingo. Cilla doesn't know me. Through the kitchen door I go.

Lia pushed off the wall and headed uptown as a plan began to form in her mind.

ELLIE

*E*llie and Julian spoke with their attorney several times throughout the remainder of the week. He advised them to stay calm and let Lia make the next move.

"Keep your doors locked and your eyes peeled," Tyler told them repeatedly. "If she was concerned about her children, she wouldn't have waited seven months to contact you. Let's hope she came to town looking for money. That would play in our favor when we try to negotiate an adoption agreement."

Their last conference call with Tyler was late Friday afternoon. Ellie sat across from Julian at the table on the terrace with her iPhone on speaker between them.

"There's still no sign of her," Ellie said about her sister. "Do you think we should go ahead with the party?"

"I see no reason not to," Tyler said. "Putting your lives on hold for her makes you a victim. Don't give your sister that power."

"I keep wondering if maybe we should contact the Key West police," Ellie said. "If for no other reason than to let them know she's here."

"But you don't know for certain she's here," Tyler argued.

Ellie and Julian agreed. In the end, they decided to wait it out, at least until after the party.

Cilla was a welcome addition to the Hagood household. Her wide smile on her plump face brightened Ellie's days. She did everything anyone asked of her and more. She scented their bed linens and towels with lavender, organized the shoes in Ellie's closet, and ironed crisp creases in Julian's khaki slacks. The girls took to her right away as well—especially the twins, who loved it when she fussed over them. Only twenty-four years old, Cilla was still a child herself. She styled their hair in elaborate braids, played hide-and-seek with them all over the house, and helped them bake cupcakes for their real birthday on Thursday.

Midafternoon on Sunday, the household was a flurry of activity as they prepared for the party. Julian and Ellie draped white linen tablecloths over rectangular tables on the terrace— one for the self-serve bar and the other for the food—while Katie and Ruby assisted Becca in setting up activity tables along the edge of the brick wall in the garden—bead stringing, face painting, and clay sculpting. Maddie shaped hamburger patties at the island in the kitchen while Cilla stood at the counter mixing ingredients for potato salad. Bella and Mya, who were beyond themselves with excitement, chased each other around, getting in everyone's way.

Promptly at four o'clock, Ellie and Julian moved to the front door to greet their first guests. Butterflies of nervousness fluttered around in Ellie's belly. She'd been married to Julian for five months, and she'd only met the few close friends he'd invited to their wedding. A continuous stream of neighborhood families, with young children from ages two to ten, strolled through the door. Ellie plastered a smile on her face. She preferred mingling in smaller crowds. She would have to get used to playing hostess for the sake of her husband, who loved to entertain.

Abbott and Lacey brought up the rear of the initial throng of people. Her father's new romantic interest bore a natural appearance—golden tan, face free of makeup, and dark hair streaked with gray pulled back in a loose ponytail at the nape of her neck.

"I'm so glad to finally meet you," Ellie said, extending her hand to Lacey. "Dad tells me you might be in the market for a part-time job."

"I am," Lacey said with a twinkle in her clear green eyes. "And I'd love to hear about your new venture."

Abbott hip-bumped Ellie out of the threshold. "You can talk about it later. Go entertain your guests. We'll greet the stragglers."

All hosts, including Maddie and Cilla, had been warned to be on the lookout for Lia.

For the next hour, Ellie mingled with her guests while keeping an eye on her girls. Her stepdaughter and foster child seemed to be adapting well to their new environment. Even so, Ellie sensed mild jealousy from Katie, who wasn't used to sharing a bathroom—or her father—with siblings, and skepticism from Ruby, who was struggling to trust the new grown-ups in her life.

As the party wore on, the guests feasted on the smorgasbord of food Maddie and Cilla set out. It was nearly six o'clock when Maddie deemed it time to cut the cake. Parents and children gathered around the twins to sing "Happy Birthday." The crowd applauded as Bella and Mya blew out the candles, but one pair of hands continued to clap long after everyone else had stopped.

Ellie searched the group for the enthusiastic guest. Her eyes fell on a woman who looked vaguely familiar standing beside the french doors leading to her studio. It took a minute for her mind to register that the face staring out at her with the condescending expression from beneath the blonde wig belonged to her sister.

Ellie crossed the terrace in three strides. Lia saw her coming and said in a voice loud enough to attract their guests' attention, "Ellie Darling, how nice of you to throw a birthday party for *my* children."

Out of the corner of her eye, she saw Bella and Mya cowering behind Maddie. "If you care about your children at all, you won't dare cause a scene in the middle of their birthday party."

Lia stepped in front of her, planting herself inches from Ellie's face. "So now you're an expert on what's best for my children?"

Ellie drew herself to her full height. "Damn straight, I am. I've been raising them for the past seven months while you've been off gallivanting God knows where."

"You offered," Lia said with an arrogant shrug of her shoulder.

"Why, you little bit—"

Julian and Abbott arrived on the scene at the same time. "Let's talk about this in private," Julian said. He held the door open for Abbott, who took Lia by the elbow and escorted her inside the house and down the hall to Julian's study.

Ellie slammed the heavy door when she entered, and the foursome stood awkwardly facing one another in the center of the room.

"How'd you get in the house, Lia?" she asked, her eyes glued on her father, who was supposed to have been manning the front door.

Abbott raised his hands in defense. "I didn't let her in. She must've gotten in some other way."

"Your new maid let me in through the kitchen door. I believe she told me her name is Cilla. She didn't recognize me in my disguise." Lia pulled the blonde wig off her head. "You should be more careful, Eleanor. I've been snooping around your house for days, and you didn't even know I was here."

Ellie's stomach heaved, and bile rose in her throat. "You're just saying that," she said, although she suspected it was true.

"How do you think I found out about your little birthday soirée for my girls? You really should watch what you say when your windows are open. I heard your naughty pillow talk. I know all about how Julian likes to—"

Julian grabbed Lia's wrist and twisted it behind her back. "Don't you dare, you—"

"Don't waste your breath, Julian. She's not worth it," Ellie said. He dropped Lia's arm.

She noticed her sister was even thinner than she'd been the last time she'd seen her back in September—if that was even possible—but her skin was bronze from hours spent on the beach.

Has she been in Key West this whole time?

"In your letter, you claimed you needed some time to find your way," Ellie said. "How does your husband's murder factor into your pathway to discovery?"

Lia jutted out her chin. "I had nothing to do with Ricky's death."

"Then how do you explain why your fingerprints were all over the light switch?" Abbott asked.

"I don't owe you any explanations," Lia said to Abbott, but her eyes remained on Ellie.

"Maybe not," Ellie said. "But you owe Detective Hamlin in Key West an explanation as to why your fingerprints were found at the scene."

"You'd like that, wouldn't you, Eleanor? To have me tucked away in jail so you can claim my children as your own. Go ahead and call Detective Hamlin." Lia thrust her cell phone at her. "What're you waiting for?"

"We're waiting to hear your side of the story," Julian said in a soft-but-firm voice.

Lia turned her attention to Julian. "I'd forgotten how handsome you are," she said, palming his cheek. "You poor, deprived man, being married to my sister, the prude. Why don't you come home with me? I'll show you a good time you won't soon forget."

Anger pulsed through Ellie's veins, and she had to work hard not to smack her sister's face. Lia was goading her, but she would not dignify her insults with a response.

Julian smacked Lia's hand away. "Not that it's any of your business, but Ellie and I are happily married. Even if we weren't, I would never be attracted to a woman like you."

"Humph," Lia said, waving her hand in dismissal. "Your loss."

Ellie crossed her arms and tapped the toe of her sandal on the carpet. "We're still waiting for your side of the story."

"Ugh, Eleanor. You really are such a bore." Lia turned her back on them and circled the room, running her hand along the marble mantel before moving to the window. "If you must know, it's a very short story. I was framed."

"By whom? The loan sharks from Georgia?" Ellie asked.

"Or Ricky's lover," Lia said, fingering the velvet on the floor-to-ceiling drapes. "You're asking all the wrong questions, you know? You should be asking what it's going to take to get rid of me."

Ellie looked at her husband, who gave her the nod. "Okay, then. I'll bite. What's it going to take to get rid of you?"

"I want what's rightfully mine." Spinning around to face the room, she spread her arms wide. "Half of all of this."

"In other words, you're broke. I figured as much. All of this wealth"—Ellie mocked her sister by spreading her arms—"has been in our family for generations. It's our responsibility to be good stewards of that money for the generations of Pringle family members yet to come. Not to squander it as you've done. I gave you a very large sum of money, and you've blown through it in seven months."

Lia crossed the room to Ellie. Her face was so close that Ellie could smell her sister's rank breath. "You asked what I want, and I'm telling you. I want half of your inheritance. In exchange, I'll let you keep my children. That's a fair deal, if you ask me."

Ellie pressed her hand against her belly as a wave of nausea hit her. "You're selling your children to me, in other words."

"They're worth it, don't you think?" Lia walked to the door.

"You have twenty-four hours to make the arrangements, or I'll take my children away from here and you'll never see them again."

Abbott rushed to open the door for her. "I'll walk you back to your hotel."

"No thanks," she said as she breezed past him. "My hotel is on the other side of town."

"Then I'll drive you," he called after her. "Ellie, where are your keys?"

"In the dish on the hall table. Be careful, Dad."

Ellie recognized her father's ulterior motive. While he was pretending to be a gentleman, a man concerned about his daughter's well-being, what he really wanted was to find out where her sister was staying.

THE PARTY GUESTS began to trickle out after Abbott left. By six thirty, all had gone home to their Sunday-night routines. Ruby and Katie had retired to their rooms, to the homework that awaited them, and Becca had whisked the now-grumpy birthday girls off to bed. Lacey helped Julian and Ellie clean up the yard while Maddie and Cilla tackled the kitchen.

Ellie and Lacey were folding a tablecloth together when Lacey said, "You may not feel like talking about this right now, but I'd love to hear more about your art gallery sometime."

Ellie took Lacey's ends of the tablecloth and folded it in half. "I was planning on talking about the gallery with you at some point. Might as well be now. I could use the diversion. I'll be honest with you, Lacey. I'm in over my head with this project. I bought the warehouse on a whim. The upstairs is perfect for my studio. I have some ideas about the gallery downstairs, but I have no idea how to implement them."

"I have some time tomorrow morning if you're free. You can show me the place and tell me your ideas."

Ellie had no idea what tomorrow held in terms of her sister. But the sooner she found someone else to worry about the gallery, the better off she'd be. "As of now, I'm free all morning. You name the time."

"How about late morning? Say around eleven."

"Eleven it is," Ellie said. "Let's go in the kitchen, and I'll write down the address."

Maddie brewed a pot of coffee, and Julian, Ellie, and Lacey gathered around the kitchen table to wait for Abbott to return.

"Took you long enough," Ellie said to her father when he arrived an hour later. "Where's her hotel, in Savannah?"

"She's staying at the Waterside Inn, which I can assure you is nowhere near the water. Roughest section of Charleston I've been in thus far." Abbott pulled a barstool close to the table and accepted a cup of coffee from Maddie. "Something's not right with her."

"That much is obvious," Ellie said. "Care to elaborate?"

"I'm talking about something different than her hitting on Julian or selling her children. She seemed so agitated on the way over to her motel. She scratched at the skin on her neck and babbled on about who knows what. She was talking so fast I couldn't understand her."

Ellie's eyes narrowed. "I can't say I'm surprised. We suspected she was unstable when we first met her in September. Louisa told us about her prior bouts with depression and attempted suicide."

"Who's Louisa?" Lacey asked.

"The woman who raised Lia," Abbott explained. "She was an old friend of Ellie's mother's."

"I see," Lacey said with a nod.

"Do you think she's in some kind of manic state?" Julian asked.

"I think there's a good chance, which is all the more reason to keep her away from the twins," Abbott said. "We decided the other day to let Lia make the next move before we called the police, but now that she has, considering the behavior I just witnessed in the car, I'm more inclined than ever to turn her in. I'm sure I don't need to remind you that you have four children living under your roof who need to be protected."

Julian locked eyes with Ellie. "I agree with your father on this."

She hesitated a long minute. "But if it backfires and Lia manages to escape the police, we'll never see her again. Can we give it one more day? We all heard her state, in no uncertain terms, she wants half of my inheritance. I'll pay her off in exchange for her signature on the adoption papers."

"Until the next time she runs out of money," Julian said.

"We'll make her sign a legal agreement stating that there will be no next time," Ellie said.

Abbott steepled his fingers. "Let's focus on the bigger picture for a minute. Forget about the money and the adoption. If she murdered her husband and we don't turn her in, who's to stop her from killing again?"

"I hear what you're saying, Dad. Just give me one more day to work my deal. Then we'll call the police. Or better yet, if we can have a reasonable conversation with her, we can convince Lia to turn herself in. She claims she was framed. Maybe she could help the police in their investigation."

Abbott slowly let out his breath. "All right, sweetheart. This is your family. I'm willing to play it your way for now. But if there's been no resolution by this time tomorrow, I'm calling the police."

LIA

*U*nable to sleep, Lia hit the sidewalk in the deserted streets of downtown. Ignoring the pain from the blisters on her feet, she walked for hours past boutiques and hotels and homes where families rested in anticipation of the coming week. It was nearly three in the morning when she found herself standing in front of her sister's house. Hadn't that been her destination all along?

The night was quiet and still, aside from the sound of a dog barking in the distance. Yellow light glowed through the living room window downstairs, but the rest of the house was pitch-dark. She gave her sister credit for turning their grandmother's house of doom and gloom into a comfortable home full of joy and laughter. Lia wasn't cut out for the mundane life. She understood that now. Her sister had inherited the maternal gene from their mother, and Lia had gotten . . . well, as much as she hated to admit it, she was more like their grandmother, wicked old bitch that she was. Her daughters would be safe here with Ellie and Julian. Being so close and unable to get to her children was torture. She knew if she held them in her arms, she'd never be able to let them go. She loved Bella and

Mya more than life itself. She was giving her girls parents who would provide for them and nurture them. Parents they could count on.

When a fresh rush of energy flowed through her, she turned her back on the antebellum mansion and headed up East Bay Street, toward her hotel. Walking at a brisk pace, she arrived at the Waterside Inn thirty minutes later. She fell into bed and slept without moving until loud knocking on the door woke her in the early afternoon.

Tossing an arm over her head, she hollered at the closed door, "Go away! I don't need maid service today."

"Police! Open up!"

Police? She sat bolt upright. *Has something happened to the twins?* She swung her feet over the side of the bed. She stood too quickly, and the sudden surge of blood to her head made her feel dizzy. She stumbled across the room and swung the door open. Two uniformed officers, both in their midthirties and handsome despite their bald heads, stood before her.

"Are you Lia Bertram?"

It dawned on her then that they might be there about Ricky's death. "Depends on who's asking."

The shorter of the two said, "I'm Officer Little, and this is Officer Owens." He elbowed his partner. "We're with the Charleston Police Department. We have a warrant for your arrest for the murder of your husband, Ricky Bertram."

A warrant? Arrest?

"On what grounds?"

"I'm not privy to the details of the case," Little said. "You can come with us of your own free will, or we can handcuff you. Your choice."

Lia's mind raced. She considered kneeing Little where it counts and darting past him, but she wouldn't get far feeling so light-headed. If she slammed the door in their faces, they'd break it down and come in after her. There was no other way out of the room anyway, no bathroom window for her to sneak out of. She was screwed. Her best bet was to go peacefully with them.

I have nothing to hide. I didn't kill Ricky. I'll tell the truth, and then maybe I can stop running.

Her shoulders slumped. "Give me a minute."

She left the door open while she located her purse and tied a scarf around her neck. As she slipped on her sandals, she noticed her feet were filthy from her midnight stroll around town.

After the inquisition, I'll treat myself to a pedicure, she thought, and then remembered she was flat broke. *Forget the pedicure. I'll cut the deal with my sister, get my money, and leave this town for good.*

The ride to the police station took twenty minutes due to the horse-drawn carriages slowing traffic at every turn in the downtown business district. Lia combed her fingers through her greasy hair, gathered it back into a ponytail, and secured it with an elastic band. She must look a wreck. She couldn't remember the last time she'd showered.

At the station, after reciting her Miranda rights, the female booking officer, who identified herself as Officer Kelly, took her mug shot and fingerprinted her. After performing a strip search, she gave Lia an orange jumpsuit to wear and placed her in a holding cell.

"What're you doing?" Lia said, her fingers gripping the metal bars. "You can't lock me up like this, without letting me make a phone call."

"Don't worry. You'll get to make your call," Officer Kelly said, but she didn't say when.

Who would she call when she got her chance? She knew only three people in town—Ellie, Julian, and Abbott—and one of them must have ratted her out to the police. Lia had made a fatal mistake. She should have suspected they would turn her in.

Lia paced the floors for what felt like hours, although she had no idea of the time. She felt naked without her scarf and scratched at her neck until the skin around her scar was raw. The concrete walls began to cave in on her, and she found it difficult to breathe. She inhaled and exhaled deeply to calm herself and steady her mind.

The waiting was excruciating, and by the time Officer Kelly returned, Lia was ready to tear her hazel eyes out.

"Come with me, please."

Handcuffing her, the officer led her out of the holding area and down several long hallways to a room with a table, four chairs, and a one-way mirror.

"I'm going crazy here, Officer. You can't keep me locked up like a caged animal."

"We can and we will." She removed Lia's handcuffs, and placing a hand on her shoulder, she forced her down into a chair. "Detective Lambert will be with you in a minute. He'll explain the situation to you."

Lia watched the seconds click off the clock. Thirty minutes passed, and then thirty more. It was four thirty before a man dressed in jeans and a knit-collared shirt entered the room and identified himself as Detective Lambert. Lia shot to her feet.

"This is BS, Detective. What grounds do you have to arrest me?"

"This is not my case, therefore I'm not privy to the details of the case." Doubt clouded her face, and he motioned her to the table. "Have a seat, Mrs. Bertram, and I'll tell you what I know."

She returned to the table, and he sat down opposite her. She estimated Lambert to be in his midforties. He was probably once a looker, before his hairline started receding and his gut grew large.

"I was told that your fingerprints were taken from the crime scene, and a witness saw you fleeing the hotel around the time of the murder, which is more than enough evidence for the judge to issue a warrant for your arrest. I've just gotten off the phone with Detective Hamlin in Key West. He's coming to Charleston to question you. Unfortunately, he can't get here until tomorrow. He considers you a flight risk and asked that we keep you overnight."

Lia's jaw hit the table. "In jail?"

"No, in the Charleston Place Hotel," Lambert said in a sarcastic tone. "Of course you'll be staying in jail. You've been arrested on suspicion of murder."

Lia sank lower in her chair. "In that case, give me my phone. I'm entitled to make a call."

ELLIE

*E*llie's nerves were like electrical currents as she race-walked to the gallery on Monday morning. Her green eyes darted up and down the streets in search of any sign of Lia. Her stomach churned. She'd declined Maddie's offer of breakfast and drank four cups of coffee instead. When two female joggers appeared suddenly from behind, she jumped out of their way and fell into the window box of the row house she happened to be passing at the time, scraping her elbow and bruising her shoulder.

She'd threatened to cancel her meeting with Lacey, but Julian had pleaded with her not to. "There's nothing you can do here except worry yourself into a frenzy." He'd already placed the call to Tyler who, according to his secretary, would be in court all day.

"But I want to be here if Lia shows up," Ellie argued. "I'm worried for the twins' safety."

"I'll stay here with them while you meet with Lacey. Trust me, Lia will not cross the threshold into this house."

Recognizing she needed the distraction, she finally said, "Okay, but promise you'll call me the minute you hear from Tyler. Or if Lia shows up."

"I promise. Now stop worrying about what's going on at home, and go hire yourself a gallery manager." Julian had patted her fanny as she exited the back door.

After a brief tour of the warehouse, Ellie offered Lacey the part-time position, and she agreed to start immediately.

She bummed a ride home from Lacey, and then ate lunch in the kitchen with the twins and Becca. The twins barely touched their ham sandwiches, so eager were they to return to the mountain of birthday gifts waiting for them in their playroom upstairs.

Ellie passed the long hours of the afternoon in her studio trying, and failing, to summon inspiration for her blank canvas. She was helping Katie with a math problem when her cell phone rang—from an unknown number. She considered ignoring the call, and then thought better of it. When she heard her sister's voice, she took the call outside to the garden.

Her sister's tone was both reckless and desperate as she launched into her diatribe. "I'm at the police department. I've been arrested for murdering my husband, which should come as no surprise to you since you're undoubtedly the one who turned me in. You need to get me a lawyer. I'll lose my mind if I have to spend more than five minutes in a jail cell."

"Back up a minute, Lia. I don't know what you're talking about. Why do you assume I'm the one who turned you in?"

"Duh! Isn't it obvious? You won't have to share your inheritance with me when the jury sentences me to death by electrocution."

Dread crawled down Ellie's spine. "Lia, I swear, it wasn't me. I'm not the one who called them."

"Liar! They arrested me this afternoon at my motel. They knew right where to find me. No one else knew I was staying at the Waterside Inn except Daddy Dearest. And I'm sure he told his darling princess, Ellie."

And Julian, Ellie thought.

Only the three of them knew Lia was staying at the Waterside

Inn. Would Julian or Abbott turn her sister in without telling her? "Look, Lia, I don't know what's going on here, but I intend to find out. Sit tight. Help is on the way."

She ended the call and placed another one to her father. When Abbott answered on the first ring, she said, "Guess where Lia is."

"I have no idea. Please tell me she's gone back to Key West."

"She's in jail," Ellie said, and listened carefully for the tone of his response.

"In jail?" He sounded genuinely surprised. "How'd that happen?"

"Why don't you tell me?"

"If you're suggesting I told the police where to find her, you're mistaken. I would never go against your wishes, Ellie. I think you know me better than that."

"I believe you, Dad." If it wasn't her father, then her husband must have been the one who told the police where to find Lia. "Can you come over?"

"I'm on my way."

Ellie was waiting for him on the sidewalk outside the garden gate when he arrived ten minutes later. Abbott engulfed her in a hug and, over his shoulder, she spotted Julian walking toward them from the opposite direction.

"Uh-oh," Julian said when he saw her concerned expression. "What's wrong?"

"Lia's been arrested for murdering her husband."

His eyes narrowed. "That's not good." He held the garden gate open for them. "Let's go in here and talk."

They filed through the gate and stood huddled together in the garden while Ellie explained the situation. "I understand why you turned her in, Julian. What I don't understand is why you didn't tell me."

He shook his head. "Hold on, Ellie. It wasn't me. I wouldn't do something like that without discussing it with you first."

They heard a sob from the vicinity of the terrace and turned at once to see Maddie, her face pinched in pain and her fist clenching the front of her dress. "It was me, Miss Ellie. I'm the one who called the police. I don't blame you if you fire me, but I did what I thought right. Miss Lia's pure evil, just like your gramma. I couldn't let her destroy those precious chil'run the way your gramma destroyed you."

With tears streaming down her cheeks, she started for the table but stumbled, catching herself before she fell. Ellie rushed to her side and helped her into a chair. "Get her some water please, Julian."

"I'm on it," Julian said, and disappeared inside.

Ellie pulled up a chair close to Maddie and stroked her arm while she cried. Abbott locked eyes with Ellie from across the table, and she interpreted his grave expression. Her housekeeper had taken it upon herself to call the police on Lia, and they, in turn, needed to take heed to her warning.

Maddie had lived through the horrors that happened in this house. She knew their history better than Lia or Ellie. Her knowledge of the past enabled her to view the situation with more experienced eyes. Ignoring Maddie's comparison of Lia to her grandmother would be foolish and dangerous. Was Lia pure evil? Ellie didn't know. But her sister's behavior suggested some type of psychological disorder. She'd abandoned her children for seven months and blown through a small fortune. If Ellie let her sister have her way, she would keep coming back for more money. Why had she been so worried about being fair to Lia when Lia had not been fair to her since the day they met? Lia wasn't her problem. The twins were her priority. The seven months that Bella and Mya had been in her care was a long time in the life of a four-year-old. For every day of those seven months, memories of their mother had grown dimmer and dimmer for them. Bella and Mya still called them aunt and uncle, but in every way that mattered, Ellie and Julian were their parents. Those sweet little girls had placed all their trust in them, and Ellie planned to honor that trust by doing everything in her power to protect them.

Julian returned with a glass of water, two aspirin, and a handful of tissues. He handed all three to Maddie and sat down next to Abbott.

Ellie rubbed her back while Maddie swallowed her aspirin and blew her nose. "You did the right thing in calling the police. I should've done it myself, but I was too busy worrying about Lia's well-being when my primary concern should've been the twins' safety." She squeezed her shoulder. "And for the record, there is absolutely nothing you could do that would ever make me fire you. You're like family to me, just as Abbott is my father. You're the closest thing to a mother I've ever had."

More tears filled Maddie's eyes, and she dabbed at them with a tissue. "That means the world to me."

"I hate to see you so upset. We need to get you home. Who drove today, you or Cilla?" Ellie asked.

"We came in my car, but I'll get Cilla to drive me home. All this stress is making me feel my age." Maddie gripped the arms of her chair as she hoisted herself up.

Ellie jumped to her feet and grabbed hold of the old woman's arm to help her up. Placing a hand at her waist for support, she walked Maddie inside to the kitchen.

"You be kind to yourself tonight," she said to Maddie. "Have Alfred cook dinner for you for a change."

That brought a smile to her face. "Oh lawd, Miss Ellie. Old Alfred is useless in the kitchen. I'd rather eat cat food than anything he make."

Ellie laughed. "Order out, then. Whatever you do, get some rest. If you need to take the day off tomorrow, just let me know."

Cilla retrieved their purses from the utility room and helped her friend out to the car.

Ellie watched them go, and then went upstairs to check on

the children. Ruby and Katie were in their respective rooms doing homework, and the twins were in their playroom with Becca watching *Winnie the Pooh*.

She found her father and husband deep in conversation when she returned to the terrace. "What're you two scheming?" she asked, reclaiming her chair.

"We're trying to figure out where we go from here," Julian said.

Abbott said, "I hope you realize, honey, that you don't owe Lia a thing. If anything, she owes you for taking care of her children all this time. Julian and I agree that I should be the one to hire the attorney for Lia."

"You don't owe her anything either, Dad. She hasn't exactly been nice to you."

"Maybe not, but I wasn't around when she was young. I feel obligated to find Lia good representation so that she can have a fair trial."

"Do we even know who to hire?" Ellie asked. "Maybe there's a criminal attorney in Tyler's group."

Her husband flashed his mischievous smile. "I do know of someone—but not in Tyler's firm."

Ellie rolled her eyes. "Of course you do. So who is he, your poker partner?"

"You know I don't play poker." Julian picked his phone up from the table. "I designed his beach house on Isle of Palms several years ago. His name is Gary Bates, and he's one of the best criminal attorneys on the East Coast." His thumbs flew across the screen as he typed. "I'm texting him now, asking him to call me as soon as he can."

While her husband typed his message, Ellie turned her attention to her father. "Thanks, Dad. Considering the custody situation with the twins, I think it's best if I stayed out of it. The estate can reimburse you for the attorney's fees."

Abbott patted her hand. "First things first. We can worry about all that later."

Julian's phone rang, and he answered the call from Gary Bates. He provided an introduction to his father-in-law and handed the phone to Abbott, who walked Bates through the events leading to Lia's arrest. Abbott was silent while he listened to the attorney. Before ending the call, he gave Bates his own number and asked him to use it going forward.

"He's going to see what he can find out and let us know," Abbott said.

Ellie's eyes sought out her husband's. "We need to talk to Tyler. Do you think he's out of court yet?"

Julian glanced at his watch. "He should be by now. I'll give him a call," Julian said as he stepped away from the table.

"Tell me what to do, Dad." Ellie's eyes were on her husband as he paced around the garden with his phone pressed to his ear. "Even if the police determine she didn't kill Ricky, she's not stable enough to raise Bella and Mya. I'm willing to pay Lia whatever she wants to get her out of their lives. But it seems irresponsible to give her a fortune for her to squander."

"Your attorney will advise you on the best way to handle the situation. But you need to fight to keep the twins *and* your money. Bring out the big guns if you have to. She's flat broke, which makes her vulnerable and gives us the upper hand. I barely know Lia, but she's still my daughter. If it turns out she's mentally ill, I will get her the help she needs, provided she's willing to accept it. If the behavior we witnessed from her yesterday continues, and it turns out she's your grandmother's reincarnation, I will run her out of town myself. And she won't be taking my granddaughters with her."

Ellie's lips turned up into a soft smile. "That's exactly what I needed to hear."

Abbott's phone rang with a call from Bates, and he snatched it up. The attorney's powerful voice boomed loud enough over the line for Ellie to hear most of what he said. The police considered Lia a flight risk, therefore they were holding her until Detective Hamlin arrived tomorrow morning from Key West. Bates would be there when they questioned her, and promised to call Abbott with updates as the situation evolved.

Julian rejoined them as Abbott was ending his call. "Tyler has to be back in court all day tomorrow, but he's agreed to meet us tonight. I booked a table at Husk for seven o'clock."

Ellie glanced at her watch. "That only gives us an hour. I don't even know if Becca can babysit."

"I'll stay with the girls," Abbott said, rising from the table. "We'll order takeout and stuff ourselves silly."

"Thank you, Abbott. That would be very helpful." Julian turned to Ellie. "Why don't we go early and have a drink? We have a lot to discuss before we meet with Tyler."

ELLIE

*E*llie quickly changed into a pale blue, sleeveless linen dress and espadrilles. After spending a few minutes with each of the girls, she and Julian headed off on foot, hand in hand, toward Queen Street. As they navigated the uneven sidewalks, they inhaled the sweet fragrances of early summer—ligustrum, magnolia, honeysuckle—the intoxicating scents that usually promised hope for a new season but did little to chase away Ellie's feelings of dread that particular evening.

"After hearing the desperation in my sister's voice, I'd do almost anything to keep Lia away from the twins," Ellie said as they waited for the pedestrian-crossing light to change at Meeting and Broad.

Julian squeezed her hand. "Let's wait and hear what Tyler has to say. The most important thing is for us to remain calm. If we go off half-cocked, we'll come across as being as unstable as Lia."

"That makes sense," Ellie agreed, and they walked the rest of the way in silence.

She located an empty table in the small courtyard while Julian went inside the renovated brick building that housed the bar for one of Charleston's most celebrated restaurants. He joined her five minutes later with two glasses of Madeira wine.

"A lot has happened in the three weeks since we flew to Key West looking for your sister. At the time, I thought Lia incapable of killing her husband." Julian looked away, watching a young couple emerge from the bar building. "I'm not so sure anymore."

"Me either." Ellie ran her fingertip along the lip of her wineglass. "More and more, I'm starting to think she's schizophrenic or has some other type of disorder. Maybe she's bipolar. I'm not a psychiatrist, and I'm not trying to diagnose her. But mental illness runs in families. And Maddie really struck a nerve today when she compared Lia to my grandmother. I trust her opinion. She remembers what happened in this house, and she knew my grandmother better than any of us. I hate to say it, and I wouldn't admit it to anyone except you, but having Lia locked up in jail for murder is the best-case scenario for us."

"I agree with you, sweetheart." Julian took a big gulp of wine and pushed back from the table. "Let's go check in with the hostess. I'd hate for her to give our table away."

When their attorney arrived fifteen minutes later, Ellie and Julian were seated at a corner table on the piazza in the old, two-story house that served as Husk's main dining room. Tyler signaled for the waitress to bring him a Maker's Mark on the rocks and sat down in the seat next to Ellie. He picked up the specials menu and fumbled in his blazer pocket for his reading glasses.

"I hope you don't mind, but I took the liberty of ordering several small plates for us," Julian said.

"Works for me." Tyler set his menu aside and removed his reading glasses. "I have a long day ahead of me tomorrow. The earlier I can get in bed, the better."

"Thank you for meeting us on such short notice," Ellie said.

"Of course. I understand from Julian that your sister has been arrested. The situation may take care of itself if the police have enough evidence for the prosecutor to press charges. If not, you need to be prepared for your next move in the event she's released from jail tomorrow." The waitress delivered his drink, and he took a sip. "Bring me up to speed on what's happened since we last spoke on the phone on Friday."

Ellie planted her elbows on the table and laced her fingers together. "Despite our best efforts to secure the house, Lia managed to crash the twins' birthday party yesterday afternoon. Julian whisked her off to his study before she could cause a scene. She demanded half of my grandmother's estate in exchange for custody of the girls."

"Did you agree to her deal?" Tyler asked.

"She gave us twenty-four hours to think about it," Ellie said. "The police arrested her this morning for murdering her husband, before she could circle back around to us."

A server appeared at their table with a loaded tray. "Good lord, Julian," Tyler said, his eyes round and wide. "Did you order one of everything on the menu?"

Julian shrugged. "Pretty much. I'm starving, and I wasn't sure what you liked."

The server placed platters of food in front of them: wood-fired oysters, beef tartare, pig's ear lettuce wraps, field pea salad, Southern-fried chicken skins, and a skillet of real cornbread.

"Can I get you anything else?" the server asked.

Julian requested another round of drinks.

The trio then passed platters around the table as they continued their discussion.

"The way I see it, you have two choices," Tyler said as he scooped a spoonful of cornbread onto his plate. "If you pay her off in exchange for her signature on the adoption papers, I advise you to be prudent about the amount you offer. From what you've told me, she's not privy to your financial statements, which means she has no concept of your net worth. Offer her more than last time to appease her, but be sure to leave room for negotiating."

Ellie nibbled a bite of fried chicken skin. "Yum, this is delicious." She finished the skin before asking, "What can we do to prevent Lia from coming back for more?"

"You already have the contingency clause in your contract. We'll have it signed by both you and your sister and notarized. However"—Tyler pointed his fork, its tines stuffed with field peas, at Ellie—"the next time your sister is broke, no document, legal or otherwise, will stop her from showing up on your doorstep, disrupting your lives, and pulling on your heartstrings for money."

Ellie set her fork down and lifted her wineglass. "You mentioned another option."

"We can try to fast-track our petition for legal guardianship. Judge Osborne is presiding over the lawsuit I'm currently trying in court. If I can get a few minutes with him to discuss your case, I may be able to convince him to order a psychiatric evaluation for your sister. That would accomplish two things. First, it would bring the case to his attention. Secondly, he might consider granting you temporary legal custody until the evaluation has been performed and he can render a decision."

"What if it backfires on us and scares Lia away?" Julian asked.

"She can't go anywhere without any money," Ellie reminded him.

"Exactly," Tyler said.

"Surely the judge will rule in our favor once he hears our story," Julian said, spearing another oyster off the serving platter. "We didn't ask for any of this to happen. Ellie did what any normal person would've done when she discovered she had a long-lost sister. She went in search of her, in the hopes of getting to know her. In return, Lia dumped her kids in our laps and took off. We've taken care of Mya and Bella all this time as though they were our own children. It's unfair of her to expect us to give them back when she's ready to be their mother again. Surely the judge will understand that."

Tyler offered Julian a sympathetic smile. "One would think. Unfortunately, the court often rules in favor of the parent despite the circumstances. You need to be prepared for that."

"Losing this case is not an option," Ellie said, thinking she sounded as desperate as her sister. "I refuse to turn those helpless children over to a potentially dangerous woman."

"It's my job to warn you of every possible outcome. With that said, I believe you stand a good chance of getting custody."

"Well, I . . ." Ellie felt pressured to voice a decision she wasn't quite ready to make. The legitimacy of getting a judge involved appealed to her as much as it scared her. Writing a check to Lia seemed so much easier. No matter how ironclad her contract, there would always be strings attached with that option. She was curious what the psychiatric exam might prove. Many mental illnesses tended to run in families, which meant one or both of the twins could one day face the challenges of a genetic mental disorder. In some ways, it was better not to know than to have that cloud hanging over them. In other ways, knowing of the threat enabled them to be better prepared. "I really need to sleep on it before I make my decision."

"Say no more." Tyler cut the air with his hand. "I'd like to give it some additional thought as well. Maybe I can come up with another option. I'm due in court at nine tomorrow morning, but I could talk anytime before that."

Ellie relaxed back in her chair. She'd sleep and pray on it. With any luck, the situation would appear clearer to her in the morning.

"Well, then," Julian said, placing his palms on the table. "Now that that's settled, shall we order some entrées or dessert?"

Tyler rubbed his belly. "Thanks, but I've had a gracious plenty. I need to get home to bed so I'll be well rested for court tomorrow." He stood and squeezed Ellie's shoulder as he rounded the table. "Hang in there. I'm confident things will work out the way they're meant to."

She smiled up at him. "I hope you're right." Once he'd left, she turned to Julian and said, "I wish I shared his confidence."

"I know what you mean," Julian said in a solemn voice. "Shall I get the check?"

"Please! I couldn't eat another bite, even if this is the best cuisine in town."

They finished their wine while waiting for the check. "I paid the deposit on the Sullivan's Island rental house today," Julian said on the way home. "Just think. In two weeks' time, all of this will be behind us. We'll spend a heavenly week at the beach with our girls. If luck is on our side, all three custody agreements will be signed, sealed and delivered, and our family will be legitimate."

"A lot of water needs to flow over the dam in a short amount of time in order for that to happen." Her breath hitched. "I haven't thought about it, Julian, but if Social Services gets wind that my sister is a murder suspect and that she poses a threat to her daughters, who happen to be living in the same house with Ruby, they could take Ruby away from us. The same goes for Katie, if Laura finds out about Lia."

Julian brought her in for a half hug. "Calm down, Ellie. You are getting way too far ahead of yourself. Nobody is taking anybody away from us. We simply won't let it happen."

"It creeps me out the way Lia was sneaking around our house. If he doesn't have the evidence to charge her with murder, Hamlin will have to release her tomorrow from jail, and she'll be free once again to spy on us."

"I'm one step ahead of you. I have a friend, Robbie Simon, who took early retirement from the police force after he was shot during a domestic dispute. What do you think about me hiring Robbie to guard the house?" Julian saw her expression of doubt and added, "Don't worry. I'll make certain Robbie's discreet and stays out of everyone's way."

"The idea of an ex-cop lurking around the house feels like an invasion of privacy. But with Lia roaming the streets, I have to admit I'd feel better knowing he was nearby. I guess we don't have much choice."

He massaged her shoulders. "I'll get in touch with him, to see if he's available."

Back at the house, they found Abbott in the living room, watching an old western. He turned off the TV when they entered the room. Ellie sat down on the sofa beside her father and Julian in the chair next to him. "I trust your meeting was productive," Abbott said.

"As well as can be expected," Ellie said, and then briefly outlined their options. "Tyler advised us not to make a rash decision. I'm going to think about it tonight and let him know in the morning what plan of action we'd like to pursue."

"I think that's wise," Abbott said. "Feel free to call me tonight or in the morning if you need to talk."

"I will, Dad. Thanks." Ellie patted her father's arm. "By the way, did Lacey tell you I hired her today?"

His face beamed. "Are you kidding me? She's so excited she can hardly talk about anything else." He glanced at the clock above the mantel. "She's at my house now, picking out the photographs for my opening. I should get home to oversee the selection."

They all stood and walked together to the door. "How were the girls?" Ellie asked.

"Delightful, as always. We ordered takeout from Toast. The girls got burgers, and I had the shrimp and grits."

"I've never eaten there," Julian said. "Is it any good?"

"It can't compare to Maddie's cooking, but it's better than pizza. You should try it sometime. They deliver."

"That's good to know," Ellie said.

"The twins have been asleep for an hour." Abbott snickered. "But I had to chase Katie out of Ruby's room three times. They're giggling and carrying on. I suspect Ruby's trying to finish her homework, but she's too considerate to ask Katie to leave."

Ellie smiled. That scenario had become their nightly routine. "That sounds about right."

"My daughter is lonely," Julian explained. "Turns out she's too social for homeschooling. The sooner her friends get out for the summer, the better off we'll all be."

They shared a laugh. "She seems happy," Abbott said. "That's the most important thing."

They bid him good night and closed the door behind him.

"Let me go see if I can dig up Robbie's number," Julian said, already on his way to his study.

Ellie was suddenly too tired to walk to the kitchen for a cup of chamomile tea. Gripping the railing, she trudged up the stairs and peeked in on the girls. Katie was snoring softly, with her right arm flung up over her head. Ruby had just finished her homework and was turning out her light. She crossed the hall to the twins' room. Wedging her body between theirs in the queen-size bed, she smoothed back their hair and kissed their sweet faces. Their peaceful presence comforted her as she replayed her conversation with Tyler over in her mind and debated her dilemma. Julian was already asleep when she finally abandoned the twins for her own bed.

She struggled with her decision well into the night. She was tempted to give Lia whatever she wanted to go away. She would, in essence, be buying her sister's children, and that felt wrong. Adopting Bella and Mya wasn't about Ellie's inability to have children of her own any more than fostering Ruby was. In the absence of competent parents, the twins needed someone to love and care for them. Julian and Ellie already did that—and could do so much more besides. What kind of stability would they have with Lia constantly coming in and out of their lives? A formal

175

adoption would give her the closure she needed, not some bogus agreement that came with a hefty price tag.

ELLIE EVENTUALLY DRIFTED off to sleep, but woke again at dawn. As the first pink rays of light streamed through her blinds, she made her decision. She would not cheapen her relationship with the twins by buying them from her sister. She would not stop fighting until that relationship was permanent in the eyes of the law.

LIA

*L*ia's skin crawled, her scalp itched, and her fingernails were bloody from clawing at the cinderblock walls. For much of the night, she'd howled like a deranged lunatic —until the guards threatened to actually send her to the psych ward at MUSC. She sent her dinner tray back untouched, and when they brought her breakfast, she sloshed the watery oatmeal all over the concrete floor and banged the plastic bowl against the metal bars. By the time the guard finally came for her at eight o'clock the next morning, Lia was on the brink of insanity.

With head bowed, she kept her eyes trained on the guard's jiggly butt as she followed her down the long row of cells and out of the holding area.

"Where are we going?" Lia asked as they walked through the maze that made up the first floor of the Charleston Police Department.

"To an interview room," Jiggly Butt said without making eye contact. "Your attorney's waiting for you."

Surprise, surprise! Lia thought. *My sister must have come through for me.*

The guard opened the door and gently shoved Lia inside the

room. A man, wearing a tailored suit that matched his gray hair and tortoiseshell horn-rimmed glasses, rose halfway out of his chair to greet her.

"I'm Gary Bates, your attorney." His eyes traveled from the top of her matted head to her feet before resting on her bloody hands. "Are you okay? You appear a little . . . disheveled."

"I had a fight with a cinderblock wall," Lia said. When a baffled expression crossed his handsome face, she added, "What can I say? I'm claustrophobic. I don't like being locked up."

"I see. Please, have a seat." He gestured at the empty chair across from him and waited for her to get settled before asking, "It's none of my business, but are you on any type of prescription medication? Considering your overnight accommodations, perhaps you missed a dose. Detective Hamlin's coming in from Florida to question you. It's important you make a good impression."

Lia glared at him. "You're right, Mr. Bates. It isn't any of your business. The only impression I need to make is one of innocence, which should be easy since I didn't kill my husband."

"Right." He picked up his phone and tapped out a text. "We still need to get you cleaned up. I'll have my secretary rush over some supplies."

"Who hired you, Mr. Bates?" Lia asked as she picked dried blood off one of her fingernails. "I hope whoever it was explained that I don't have any money to pay you."

"Your father hired me. Julian Hagood referred him to me, which is all the assurance I need that I'll get paid." He flipped open a leather folder and poised his pen over a yellow legal pad. "We don't have much time, Mrs. Bertram. Detective Hamlin will be here within the hour. Tell me as much as you can as quickly as you can."

"Fine, but call me Lia. As soon as possible, I'm ditching my husband's last name." She sat back in her chair, crossed her arms over her chest, and allowed her mind to travel back to the last point in her marriage when she could remember being happy—a few months before the twins were born.

"While my marriage had been on the rocks for years, our real problems started last September in Decatur, Georgia, where I lived with my husband and twin three-year-old daughters. May I stand? My ass is tired of sitting."

"By all means," Bates said, gesturing at the floor.

She rose from the chair and paced back and forth beside the table while she told him about her husband's financial trouble, his sudden disappearance, and the goons who showed up looking for him. She told him about Ellie and Abbott and their untimely arrival on the scene. "I had no contact with my husband for seven months until he texted me to come to Key West. He wanted to meet with me to talk about our future."

"Were these texts from the same phone number he had when you were together?"

"Nope." Lia stood in front of the one-way mirror and blew whoever was watching a kiss. "The texts were from a new number. I didn't think it strange at the time. He was on the run from bad men who he owed a lot of money. It made sense that he would have gotten a new phone."

"Are these texts still on your phone?"

With an annoyed sigh, Lia turned away from the mirror. "Yep, but they took my phone."

Bates jotted something on the legal pad in front of him. "Tell me about the texts."

"I received the first one five days before my husband was murdered. On May fifth. I remember the date. I was drinking margaritas at a Cinco de Mayo party with my then-boyfriend, Justin, when I received it."

"You're awfully trusting to assume this text was from your estranged husband without proof."

"I didn't need proof. He used his pet name for me. No one else knows it. At least that's what I thought at the time." She rolled her eyes. "I was Venus to him, his love goddess. Wonder if his new goddess is Aphrodite."

Ignoring her sarcasm, Bates asked, "And you just jumped on the next plane to Key West?"

"The next bus, actually." She dropped back down in her chair. "I'd grown tired of my boyfriend and was looking for an excuse to leave him."

"How did you know where to find Ricky once you got to Key West? Did he mention where he was staying in the texts?"

"We went to Key West on our honeymoon. I took a chance that he would be stupid enough to stay in the same place. Turns out I was right. I didn't tell Ricky I was in town. I spied on him, hoping to find out why he wanted to meet with me so I would know what approach to take. When I saw him with his new girlfriend, I figured he was going to ask me for a divorce so he could be with her. Which was fine by me. Good riddance, Ricky, as far as I was concerned. Except that custody of our twin daughters was an issue. They turned four last week."

Jiggly Butt interrupted them to announce the arrival of Bates's secretary, who was waiting outside in the hallway.

The secretary, an efficient matronly type, carried an over-stuffed canvas tote full of supplies. Jiggly Butt escorted Lia and the secretary down the hall to the ladies' restroom. After washing her face, Lia scrubbed the blood from her hands and raked a brush through her tangled hair. She slipped off her soiled T-shirt and tugged on the white cotton sweater the secretary handed her.

Detective Hamlin had arrived by the time she returned to the interview room. His golden tan gave him away. She considered him a hottie—under different circumstances, she might have hit on him.

After a round of introductions, they sat down together at the table. "We've been searching for you for some time." Hamlin offered her an insincere smile. "You're a difficult woman to find."

Her smile reflected his. "It seems you were looking in all the wrong places, Detective."

"Apparently so." He opened a manila file in front of him. "Let's get started, then. Your case has logistical challenges, since you were arrested in South Carolina for a crime you're suspected of committing in Florida. I'm here to determine if there's enough evidence to extradite you back to Florida. In the interest of time, why don't you tell me your side of the story?"

Lia gawked. "Again? I just told Mr. Bates most of it."

"You may have to tell it again and again before we're through," Hamlin said. "Start at the beginning, please."

"Ugh! Whatever." For the next thirty minutes, she walked him through the previous four years, including the events leading up to her husband's murder. Hamlin attempted, unsuccessfully, to poke holes in her story along the way. Her responses were all honest, because she was telling the truth.

When she was finished, he said, "Let's go back to the part where you left your children in your sister's care. How long did you stay in Charleston before you left?" Hamlin asked.

"Hmm." Lia cocked her head to the side and stared up at the ceiling. "A few days."

Hamlin's eyeballs popped out of their sockets. "Let me get this straight. You left your three-year-old children with a woman you'd only known for a few days?"

"Have you met my sister, Detective?"

"I have," he said. "When she flew to Key West, looking for you."

"Then you know she's the quintessential mommy."

"I can see where that would be true about her, although I would never render such a character assessment until I've known a person for much longer." His accusatory tone hung in the air and sent a message that was loud and clear: he was condemning her for abandoning her children with a woman she barely knew.

"Ellie has a big house, plenty of money, and servants to take care of Mya and Bella. Plus, our father lives nearby."

They moved on to talk about the first text she'd received from her husband, her trip to Key West, and the subsequent days of her spying on him from his hotel lobby that followed.

"Tell me about the night of the murder," Hamlin said.

Lia clasped her hands together to stop them from trembling. "My husband asked me to meet with him in his hotel room at nine o'clock that night. I found him dead when I got there. It's as simple as that."

The detective exhaled a breath of frustration. "Maybe so. But I need details."

Lia stared at her hands as that awful memory came back to her. "There was a bad storm that night, and I was running late because of the weather. I arrived at his hotel about five minutes after nine. I walked through the lobby and rode the elevator to the third floor. When I located his room, room number 550, I noticed his door ajar. I knocked, but no one answered. I pushed it open, and when I stepped over the threshold, I sensed something was not quite right. Maybe it was the smell. I don't know. I can't say for certain. I reached for the light switch. When my fingers came into contact with what I now know was blood, it surprised me. I reached for the doorknob for support—if you're wondering how my fingerprints got on the knob. Concerned for Ricky's safety, I walked farther into the room and found him dead in a pool of blood, with a knife sticking out of his heart."

Hamlin looked up from his writing. "Was he wearing any clothing?"

Lia's jaw dropped. "Why does that matter?"

"It matters in determining his activities at the time of his death."

"Of course he was fully clothed. He was dressed for a meeting with me. But you already know that, don't you?"

Ignoring her question, Hamlin returned his gaze to his notepad. "Can you describe the knife?"

"It had a black handle, like the kind professional chefs use."

His pen flew across the notepad as he wrote. "What happened then?"

"What do you think happened? I freaked out. I got the hell out of there as fast as I could."

"At any point in time did you consider contacting the police?"

"Nope. And before you ask me why, I'll tell you. My first thought was, the loan sharks he owed a bunch of money had killed him and would come after me next. But later, when I got back to my room and had a chance to process what had happened, I realized that somebody, for whatever reason, may have been framing me."

Hamlin sat back in his chair and tapped his pen against the table as he studied her. "Why do you think you were framed?"

"Because I stumbled into my estranged husband's hotel room only minutes after he was murdered. That's a little bit of a coincidence, don't you think?"

Hamlin leaned across the table toward her, staring deep into her eyes. "Who do you think was framing you?"

"The woman Ricky was sleeping with, who else?"

"What motive would she have had to kill her boyfriend and frame you?" Hamlin's face was so close to hers she smelled coffee on his breath.

"I have no idea. You're the detective. Why don't you tell me?"

"I've questioned Carrie Doyle extensively," Hamlin said. "You have more motive to kill your husband than she does."

Lia's heart pounded against her rib cage. She couldn't tell if he was bluffing. "What motive could I possibly have—aside from the fact that he walked out on me, leaving me with thirty dollars in my bank account and a platoon of goons harassing me?"

"His million-dollar life insurance policy, for starters."

Lia froze. It took her thirty seconds to recover. "I don't know what you're talking about. Am I the beneficiary to this million-dollar life insurance policy?"

"You are, according to Ricky's brother, Joey. He should know. He sold him the policy."

"I promise you, if I'd known that bastard had a million-dollar life insurance policy, I would have killed him with my bare hands while we were still living together."

Bates rested his hand on her arm, cautioning her to tread lightly. "Let's start over from the top."

"You've gotta be kidding me!" Lia sprang from her chair with eyes wild and face flushed red. "I can't stay in this room another minute. You don't have enough to press formal charges against me, because I didn't kill my husband." She strode across the room and began pounding on the door. When no one came, she moved to the one-way mirror. Banging her fist against it, she hollered over and over for someone to let her out. Finally, spent, she slid to the floor in a heap and sobbed.

Bates and Hamlin looked at each other, and Hamlin gestured for Bates to go to her.

"Why don't we take a break?" Bates suggested as he helped Lia to her feet. "Lia, can I get you some water?"

She nodded. "And I'd like to use the restroom."

She took her time in the restroom. When she returned to the interrogation room, Lambert and Bates were standing outside in the hallway. Hamlin was nowhere to be seen. She sipped her water at the table while eavesdropping on Detective Lambert and Bates, who were talking loud enough outside the open door for her to hear. Based on their conversation, she deduced that Lambert had been listening from the other side of the two-way mirror during Hamlin's questioning.

"She's a nutcase, that one," Lambert said.

In his dignified tone that hinted at money and breeding,

Bates said, "If ever there was a legitimate opportunity for a temporary insanity plea, this would be it."

"We found an empty bottle of lithium when we searched her hotel room yesterday," Lambert said. "Wonder how long it's been empty."

"I'm not surprised, considering the behavior we just witnessed," Bates said. "Interestingly enough, I asked her if she was on prescription medicine."

"Based on the dosage and the date the prescription was filled, she was taking lithium at the time of the murder but ran out shortly thereafter. She may have had it refilled since then, but we didn't find any pill bottles in her handbag. The murder took place two and a half weeks ago. If she was prescribed lithium for bipolar disorder, she could be in a manic state."

How dare the bastards search my room. They want to see manic? I'll show them manic if they don't let me out of here soon.

THE INTERROGATION RESUMED and dragged on for hours. Hamlin repeated the same questions, and she supplied the same answers. Just when Lia thought they were nearing the end, Hamlin took her down the hall, hooked her up to a lie detector test, and started all over again. They asked things about her personal life that she considered inappropriate and irrelevant to the case. Lia surprised them by answering in detail, with a smug smile on her face.

Teach them to pry into a woman's private business.

Three more agonizing hours ticked off the wall clock before Hamlin concluded he had insufficient evidence to extradite her.

"I'll speak to Detective Lambert, and we'll see what we can do to get you out of here."

Lia shot to her feet. "How long will that take?" As much as

she wanted answers, her desire to get out of that interview room was greater.

Hamlin stood to face her. "Just a few minutes." He left the room, and five minutes later, Jiggly Butt arrived to escort her to discharge to fill out paperwork and collect her belongings. Hamlin and Bates were waiting for her in the main lobby fifteen minutes later when she returned.

Bates wished her well with the shake of a hand, and Hamlin said, "I'm headed to the airport. Can I give you a lift back to your hotel on the way?"

Lia gave him the once-over, her eyes lingering on his wedding band. She'd already ruined Ricky's marriage to his first wife. She wasn't interested in a repeat performance, no matter how hot he was. And he was definitely hot, with sandy curls and a muscular bod. But she drew the line at banging a cop. On the other hand, the ride to her hotel would give her a chance to get her answers.

"Sure. Why not?" she said, and followed him out to his compact rental car in the parking lot.

Lia waited until the police station was in their rearview mirror before broaching the subject. "So, Detective, who do you think killed my husband?"

He lifted his hand off the steering wheel as if to say, "Your guess is as good as mine . . ."

"My guess is, the loan sharks finally caught up with him."

"Why not Carrie Doyle?" Lia asked.

"She remains a person of interest, but I don't think she did it. She was in love with your husband. She wanted to marry him, but Ricky was taking his time in asking you for a divorce. She pushed him along by purchasing a disposable phone and texting you. She confessed her intentions when Ricky spotted you spying on him from behind a potted plant. She arranged the meeting and told him she'd leave him if he didn't meet with you."

"Does she have an alibi for the night of the murder?"

"She does. She was in the lounge in the hotel lobby, having a drink at the bar. The bartender has corroborated her story. She stepped outside to have a cigarette seconds before you exited through the side door. She suspected something was wrong when you blew past her."

"I was in such a hurry to get out of there." Lia thought back to that night. She knew the hotel floor plan by heart by then. Instead of waiting for the elevator, she ran down the hall to the stairs. She exited the building through the side door nearest the staircase, and raced down the gravel path to the front of the hotel. "I don't recall seeing anyone."

"Security footage from the hotel confirms Doyle's story." He drummed his fingers on the steering wheel as he waited for a group of students on foot to clear the intersection. "Your husband was bludgeoned multiple times with a butcher knife. Whoever killed him would've undoubtedly been covered in his blood. Carrie Doyle is willing to testify that she got a good look at you, and there were no bloodstains on your clothing. She's the primary reason I've decided not to press charges against you."

"I'll be sure to send her a thank-you note. What happened after she saw me? Did she go inside to check on her *lover*?" Lia said, her tongue lingering on the last word.

"She said Ricky had been skittish during the week prior to his death. He was convinced someone was following him. Someone other than you. When she discovered his body, she freaked out, packed her bags, and left the hotel. Like you, she feared the goons chasing him would come after her. She's a very wealthy woman, with considerable interests to protect."

"So she has money," Lia said. "I figured as much."

They inched along in the early rush-hour traffic for several blocks. "What's next for you?" Hamlin asked.

"I'm going to pack my things, pick up my kids, and start a new life with the proceeds from my husband's million-dollar life insurance policy."

"I don't understand the ins and outs of your relationship with

187

your sister, but go easy on her. I had the opportunity to spend some time with her in Key West when she came looking for you. She's a nice lady. I believe she genuinely cares about your daughters. It won't be easy for her to give up the twins. In her condition, I—"

"What condition?" Lia asked, her head jerking toward him.

"You know . . . with the baby and all." He took his eyes off the road to study her face. "You don't know, do you?"

"Know what? Are you trying to say my sister is pregnant?"

He nodded. "At least she was when she came to Key West, nearly three weeks ago." Hamlin turned on his blinker and pulled into the parking lot of the Waterside Inn.

Lia reached for the door handle. "Great! Now that Eleanor's having a child of her own, she can stop playing mommy to mine."

ELLIE

*E*llie spent the day on Tuesday busying herself with work to keep her mind off her troubles with her sister. She met with Lacey at the gallery in the morning. She found her new gallery manager efficiently organized, full of creative ideas, and well connected in the local art world. They brainstormed ideas for future openings and discussed at length their desired ambience for the showroom. Ultimately, they agreed a contemporary minimalist style would best showcase the art. Ellie nodded her approval as Lacey suggested oriental rugs in muted colors on the brick floors and rectangular benches upholstered in white-tufted leather positioned in front of the art for patron viewing.

She arrived home in time to join her family—minus Ruby, who was at school—in the kitchen for lunch. Maddie presented them with a smorgasbord of food—a tray of assorted sandwiches, leftover cold salads from the birthday party, and a bowl of fresh fruit. In Ellie's absence that morning, Julian had interviewed and hired Robbie Simon, who had recently completed another job and was free to start protecting their house right away. They invited him to join them for lunch, and he gathered with them at the table and participated in their conversation like an old friend.

In his late fifties, Robbie appeared in excellent physical shape aside from a limp that was a result of the gunshot wound to his back. No one mentioned, and thankfully the twins appeared not to notice, the handgun holstered under his arm.

Julian left for a meeting with a client shortly after lunch, and the others retreated to their various corners of the house. Becca took the twins upstairs for their nap while Katie settled in her room to write a report on a novel she'd finished reading that morning. Ellie reluctantly retired to her studio to put the final touches on a painting she didn't much care for of the Cooper River Bridge.

Robbie declared the settee in the front hall the ideal location from which to guard the house. Every fifteen minutes, like clockwork, Ellie heard the rubber soles of his orthopedic shoes squeak against the hardwood floor as he patrolled the downstairs for signs of intruders. Never mind the only intruder they were worried about was currently in jail.

Ellie was frantic when three o'clock rolled around with no word from Bates or Hamlin regarding Lia's interrogation. She emerged from her studio and listened for sounds of life. But the house was silent. The children were still upstairs, and Maddie and Cilla had gone home early to prepare for a baby shower they were hosting for a young woman from their church. She went to the kitchen and brewed a cup of chai tea. She was slurping her first sip when she heard voices in the front hall. She emerged from the kitchen to find her father showing his driver's license to Robbie.

"It's okay, Robbie. He's my father," Ellie said, and made the introductions.

Robbie bowed his head at her. "Yes, ma'am. Sorry for the inconvenience."

She flashed him a smile. "No worries. I know you're just doing your job. Your presence is of great comfort."

Ellie walked her father back to her studio. "Have you heard anything from Bates or Hamlin?"

"Not a word." The instant the words parted his lips, his phone rang in his pocket. "I'm here with my daughter," he said to Bates. "I'm going to put you on speakerphone." Abbott and Ellie sat down side by side on the sofa, with the phone on the coffee table in front of them.

"How'd the interrogation go?" Abbott asked.

"Detective Hamlin was very thorough, which is why it took so long. He concluded there isn't enough evidence against Lia for a prosecutor to press charges. She's just been released. Hamlin is giving her a ride back to her hotel on his way to the airport."

Ellie fell back against the velvet sofa cushions as the enormity of his words struck her. Lia was once again on the loose.

"Hamlin and I had a chance to speak in private before they left the station," Bates continued. "He's going to call you after he drops Lia. In the meantime, I wanted you to be aware of Lia's somewhat volatile state of mind."

Ellie shot her father a concerned look. "That doesn't sound good," Abbott said.

"She got emotional several times during the interrogation. When I say *emotional*, I'm talking about more than a few tears. At one point, she broke down completely. I was worried we wouldn't be able to continue, but she was able to pull herself together. The police discovered an empty bottle of lithium when they searched her hotel room. You may or may not know that lithium is typically prescribed for people suffering from bipolar disorder. If she took the medicine as prescribed, beginning on the date the prescription was filled, Lia would have been on the medication at the time of Ricky's death but would've run out a day or two afterward. We found no other prescription pill bottles, either in her room or among her personal possessions when she was arrested."

"Which means, for whatever reason, she's taken herself off the lithium," Abbott said.

"Which explains her nearly manic state when she showed up at the twins' birthday party on Sunday," Ellie added.

"Which makes her a threat to herself as well as your family," Bates said.

"We appreciate the heads-up, Mr. Bates," Ellie said. "My husband has hired a retired police officer to protect us until we work things out with my sister."

"I'm glad to hear it," Bates said. "I hope you won't be needing my services as a criminal attorney going forward, but you have my number if I can be of assistance in the future."

They thanked Bates profusely and hung up. Less than a minute passed before Ellie's phone vibrated on her desk beside them, from a number with a Key West area code. She snatched up her phone and accepted the call on speaker.

"Ellie, this is Danny Hamlin. I just dropped your sister off at her motel and wanted to report to you before I leave town."

"It's nice to hear your voice, Detective," Ellie said. "My father's here with me. I hope you don't mind being on the speak-erphone."

"Of course not."

"I understand from Gary Bates that you're not pressing charges against my sister."

"That's correct. I'm convinced that Lia's not our killer. We'll continue our investigation, but we may never solve the case. It's hard to pin a murder on the likes of the people he owed money." Hamlin coughed, clearing his throat. "In any event, I wanted to warn you to be on the lookout for your sister. She seemed genuinely surprised to learn about her husband's life insurance policy. On the ride to her motel, when I asked her what was next for her, she said, and I quote, 'I'm going to pack my things, pick up my kids, and start a new life with the proceeds from my husband's million-dollar life insurance policy.' She's on a mission, Mrs. Hagood. I hate to say it, but she didn't seem at all concerned about your feelings regarding the situation."

"I expected as much, and we're prepared to handle the situation." Ellie paused. "Thank you, Detective. I appreciate your honesty and concern. I wish you the best."

She hung up and flung her phone down on the sofa as if to punish it. "That's it, Dad. We're going to lose the twins. The one thing tying us to Lia was money. Now that she will receive proceeds from Ricky's life insurance policy, there's nothing stopping her from taking Bella and Mya away from us. You do realize we'll never see them again, don't you?" Ellie left the sofa and went to stand by the windows. She stared across the yard at the magnolia tree where she'd sought refuge from her abusive grandmother as a child.

Where will my nieces hide when their mother gets out of control? What kind of life will those poor children lead with a bipolar mother as their only parent?

Ellie felt her father's presence beside her and looked up to see a tear spill from his eyelid and stream down his cheek. "I don't know about you, but I refuse to give up. I will not willingly turn my granddaughters over to Lia, even if she is their mother and my daughter. She is unfit to take care of herself, let alone two four-year-old children. We'll barricade the front door if need be. Lia will take those children out of this house over my dead body."

When she felt her father's body tremble, Ellie placed her arm around his waist. "You mean over *our* dead bodies. I don't expect you to make the same sacrifice. Not when you're beginning a relationship with Lacey. But I'm prepared to take Bella and Mya out of the country if necessary."

Abbott sucked in an unsteady breath. "That's taking matters too far, sweetheart. For you, anyway. You have Julian and Katie and Ruby to consider. Let me take them. I'm an old man. I have less to lose than you."

Her ears perked up, and she turned away from the window when she heard her husband's excited voice drifting down the hallway from the front of the house.

"Maybe he has good news."

Before she could reach the door, it swung open and Julian entered the room. "I just got off the phone with Tyler. The judge has agreed to hear our petition for adoption on Thursday morning."

LIA

*L*ia inserted her plastic card in the key card lock, turned the knob, and pushed. But the door wouldn't budge. She tried again. Instead of flashing green, the key card lock blinked red. She was locked out of her room. She'd only paid through Sunday night. Her plan had been to check out on Monday, get her money from Ellie, and leave town on the next airplane headed to Tahiti. She imagined the team of police officers who had swarmed this fine establishment as they tore through her room. Not a good way to get on the good side of motel management.

Lia marched down to the motel office and slammed her key card on the counter. "I've been locked out," she said to the fat redneck who had made a pass at her the night she checked in. "Room number 210."

He consulted his computer. "You left without paying."

"My trip was courtesy of the Charleston Police Department. My husband was murdered in Florida. Naturally, they wanted to interrogate me. Given the situation, some courtesy would be appreciated." She stretched the truth to elicit sympathy, but she could tell by his bored expression that it wasn't working.

He jabbed his thumb at his chest. "Don't look at me. I only work here."

"Naturally," Lia said with a grunt. "Where's my stuff?"

He went into the back room and returned with her suitcase. She snatched up its handle and stormed out of the office. She took off down the sidewalk, wheeling her suitcase behind her. She had nowhere to go and not a penny to her name. Correction. She had a million dollars to her name. She just had to figure out how to access it. Joey had sold Ricky the life insurance policy, but considering how much he hated her, contacting him would be her last resort. Surely, she would find a copy of the life insurance policy among Ricky's things in their home in Decatur.

For the first time since she left Georgia, she thought about their house on Cherry Blossom Lane. What a cheerful name for such a depressing place. It wasn't the house itself as much as the circumstances of her life during the time she'd lived there: marriage on the rocks, no friends, saddled with babies. Twins, no less. What had happened to their house and her husband's construction company in their absence? She'd been gone for nearly eight months and had never provided a forwarding address. Ricky had used his construction company as collateral for a bank loan to pay back some of his gambling debts.

Does that mean the company is bankrupt? Was it possible that disgruntled clients had filed lawsuits against us? Will I be forced to settle those suits with my million dollars?

Ricky had borrowed against their house as well. Had the bank foreclosed on it and auctioned off all of their possessions in her absence? She didn't care so much about the furniture and the worthless art adorning the walls. The only thing that mattered to her was the file in her husband's desk drawer marked "Life Insurance Policy." If—and that was a big if—there actually was such a file in her husband's desk drawer.

Slowing her pace, Lia window-shopped the boutiques and stores along King Street. Designer shoes and handbags. Slinky dresses that would show off her shapely legs. Diamonds and gold jewelry. Soon she'd be able to buy anything she wanted. If she managed it properly, the money would last a long time. She would travel again, to places she hadn't visited with Justin. But this time she'd remember the fine hotels where she stayed, the people she met, and the food she ate. She could go anywhere her heart desired. Footloose and fancy-free. Lia stopped dead in her tracks.

Ellie Darling was pregnant with her own prince or princess. Which made Bella and Mya second string. Lia couldn't have that. The insurance policy changed everything. She could keep the twins if she wanted to. But did she really want to go back to wiping fannies, giving baths, and planning meals? Nursing them when they were sick and listening to them whine when they were tired? And how did they fit into her travel plans? They would start school next year. She'd have to buy a small house somewhere and settle down. They would need new wardrobes every season, at the rate they grew. She saw her cash flow diminishing right before her eyes. Forty-eight hours ago, she'd been negotiating a trade with her sister—the twins in exchange for Lia's half of their grandmother's estate. Not because she didn't love her girls, but because she couldn't live without money.

Her blood pulsed through her body, surging her onward. She walked all the way down King Street to the seawall. The unanswered questions spun around inside her head, and by the time she stopped in front of Ellie's front door, she was more confused than ever about her future. As she clanged the brass knocker, she had no clue what she'd say to her sister. Only it wasn't Ellie who opened the door, but some old dude wearing a pistol in a shoulder holster.

"I need to see my sister," Lia said, barging past him.

"I'm sorry, ma'am," the gun dude said. "Mrs. Hagood isn't available at the moment."

"Like hell she isn't." Lia cupped her hands around her mouth.

"Eleanor Darling, come out, come out, wherever you are," she sang in a loud voice, her words echoing throughout the grand hallway.

"I'm going to have to ask you to leave. There are children asleep in this house." The gun dude took hold of her elbow and dragged her toward the door.

"Let go of me." Lia jerked her elbow free and yelled louder, "I'm warning you, Eleanor, I'm not going away until we settle some things."

The door to her sister's study flung open, and Ellie charged down the hall toward her with Julian and Daddy Dearest on her heels.

"Shh!" Ellie said, her finger pressed to her lips. "The girls are taking a nap."

Lia lowered her voice, but only slightly. "I thought you were avoiding me. And avoiding me would be a bad move on your part."

Ellie marched to a halt in front of Lia, with Julian and Abbott flanking her on either side.

"If these two are your bodyguards, who's the old man with the gun?" Lia aimed her thumb over her shoulder at the dude behind her.

"What do you want, Lia?"

"Well, let's see." Lia rubbed her chin between her thumb and forefinger. "First of all, I learned an interesting piece of information from Detective Hamlin today. He told me you're pregnant. And here I thought you were too old to have children."

The color drained from Ellie's face. "Not that it's any of your business, but I had a miscarriage."

The revelation caught Lia off guard, and it took her a moment to regain her composure. "I see. What a pity for you."

The gun dude stepped forward. "Would you like for me to show your sister out, Mrs. Hagood?"

"I can handle this, Robbie, but thank you," Ellie said,

offering him a sweet smile.

How Lia hated that smile.

"I'm warning you, Lia," Abbott said. "You're way out of line."

"Sorry, Daddy Dearest, but I'm just getting started." She shot Abbott the death glare before returning her focus to Ellie. "We can make the situation work in both our favors. Since you won't be giving birth to your own little prince or princess, I'll allow you to continue playing mommy to Mya and Bella in exchange for my share of the inheritance."

Julian leaned in close to Ellie. "This is counterproductive, honey. Let the judge work it out."

Lia stiffened. "What judge? What're you talking about?"

"We've petitioned the court to legally adopt Bella and Mya," Julian said. "He's agreed to hear the case on Thursday."

"Too bad I won't be sticking around to hear his decision. Go!" She snapped her fingers in Ellie's face. "Fetch my children. I'll be taking them home now."

Julian grabbed her wrist and brought her arm down to her side. "That's not happening. You can't remove them from our custody without approval from the judge."

"Says who?"

"Says the law," Julian said.

Lia suspected he was bluffing, but she decided not to push it. "Well. If that's the case, get your guest room ready, because I'm moving in." She kicked the suitcase on the floor at her feet for emphasis.

"Over my dead body," Julian said.

"Dead is not how I want to see you, Julian." She eyed him up and down. "Naked would be my choice."

Ellie's palm came out of nowhere, landing a blow on the side of Lia's cheek.

Her hand shot to her cheek. "Why, you little bitch!" Lia went after her sister with fists flinging. The dude with the gun tried to stop her, but she elbowed and kicked him out of the way. She managed to claw Ellie's neck with her fingernails and yank a handful of hair from her head before the sound of a child screaming got her attention and made her stop.

All eyes traveled to the back of the hallway, to the adolescent child who stood frozen in place with tears streaming down her face.

"Well now," Lia said. "If it isn't the red-headed foster child. It's not enough for my sister to kidnap *my* children. She has to take strays off the street as well."

When the child dashed up the stairs, Ellie took off behind her.

Julian crossed the hall in three determined strides and flung open the door. "Get out!" he demanded. "You are not welcome here."

Lia hunched her shoulders. "But I have no money and nowhere to go."

Abbott took her suitcase with one hand and her elbow with the other and marched Lia out the front door and down the sidewalk to his car. He tossed her suitcase in the trunk and shoved her in the passenger seat.

"You're a piece of work, you know that?" he said as he slid behind the steering wheel.

"I'll take that as a compliment."

"It wasn't meant to be a compliment." He started the engine. "Where to? The train or the bus station?"

"Hell no!" Lia stomped her foot against the floorboard. "I'm not leaving town without my kids. It's too late to go anywhere today anyway."

He hesitated before putting the car in gear. "Fine. I'll pay for one night, and one night only, at a hotel. After that, you're on your own."

"Can I at least have an upgrade? The last place I stayed in was a dump."

"Don't hold your breath." He stepped on the accelerator and

sped off down the block.

As he flew through the streets of downtown, Lia felt herself beginning to tank. Even though it'd been a long time since she'd experienced the dark loneliness of depression, she knew the feeling all too well. By the time they reached the Days Inn on Meeting Street, she'd bottomed out.

He retrieved her suitcase from the trunk, and they entered the motel office together. "One room for one night, please." Abbott gave his credit card to the clerk, a haggard-looking man with a braided ponytail hanging midway down his back. The clerk processed his credit card and handed Abbott a packet of key cards.

"Number 260. Last room at the end of the corridor on the second floor."

As Abbott bounced her suitcase up the single flight of concrete steps and down the exterior corridor to her room, Lia dragged herself along behind him, the energy draining from her body with each step. He unlocked the door to her room. Setting her suitcase on the floor inside, he opened his wallet and gave her all the cash he had.

"Do us all a favor and catch the next bus, train, or plane headed out of town. You and I both know you are not fit to parent those children. Get yourself some help, Lia. Believe me, you need it."

"Go to hell, Abbott." She slammed the door in his face and spun around to face the dingy room. Everything was brown— carpet, walls, and bedspread. She glanced down at the wad of cash in her hand.

Leave town, hell. Daddy Dearest is going home to a nice supper with Ellie Darling in her big fancy house with my children. It's gonna take more than a few hundred dollars to get rid of me. I'll deal with them tomorrow after I get some rest.

She collapsed onto the bed fully clothed and fell into a deep sleep.

ELLIE

*R*uby was lying facedown, crying into her pillow when Ellie entered the room.

"Oh, honey," she said as she sat down on the bed beside her. "I'm so sorry. My sister didn't mean to hurt your feelings. She's mad at me and took her anger out on you."

"Sisters aren't supposed to fight," Ruby cried, her words muffled by the pillow. "They're supposed to love each other."

"No one gets along all the time," Ellie said, rubbing circles on the child's back. "Not siblings or friends or husbands and wives. My sister and I disagree about where the twins should live. In healthy relationships, each party has to compromise in order to reach an agreement. Sadly, my sister is having some emotional problems right now, which is why we need a judge to make the decision for us. Does that make sense?"

"Sorta." Ruby rolled over onto her back. "She's mean, like mama's boyfriend. I got scared when I saw her hitting you. I didn't want her to hurt you."

"Of course you were scared, sweetheart." She took Ruby's hand in hers and brought it to her lips. "Julian and I are not the kind of people who solve our problems with our fists. In all my life, until today, I've never been in a physical fight, and I will not allow it to happen in this house ever again. We want you to feel safe here. That's why we hired a security guard. Robbie is looking out for us."

"Then why didn't he stop your sister from hitting you?"

"Because none of us realized Lia would do something like that. He'll be better prepared the next time." Ellie saw the look of horror on Ruby's face at the mention of a next time. "If there is a next time, which I doubt very seriously if my father has anything to do with it. Okay?"

Ruby smiled. "K."

Ellie leaned over and kissed her freckled forehead. "Julian and I love you very much. I want you to know you're as much a part of this family as Katie and the twins."

"Really?" Ruby beamed.

Ellie placed her hand over her heart. "Truly."

Once they'd sorted out this mess with the twins, she planned to look into a more permanent arrangement for Ruby with her family. She decided not to mention it to Ruby for fear of getting her hopes up. Not until she had a chance to discuss it with Julian and their attorney.

She patted Ruby's knee. "Why don't you get started on your homework while I go check on things downstairs?"

"Okay." Ruby sat up and swung her legs over the side of the bed. "I don't know much about these things, Miss Ellie, because I'm just a kid, but family is family. You're good at helping people. Look what you've done for me and the twins. Maybe if you help your sister fix whatever's wrong with her emotions, she'll be a nicer person."

"You know what, Ruby? I think you're right." She mussed the child's orange hair. "And kid or no kid, I think you're pretty darn smart."

Rising from the bed, Ellie smoothed the wrinkles in her linen slacks and forged a smile as she exited the room. Becca was in the hallway, hovering behind the twins' bedroom door. "Is everything okay?" She eyed Ellie's neck. "I heard yelling and was afraid to come out."

Ellie fingered the scratches on her neck. "My sister was here stirring up trouble again, but everything is under control now. Did the twins hear the argument?"

"No, ma'am. They slept right through it. They're awake now, though. Is it safe to bring them down for a snack?"

"I'd rather you keep them in their room for a few more minutes while I get cleaned up and check on things downstairs. I'll let you know when it's okay to come down." She started toward her bedroom, then turned back to face Becca. "I seem to be asking this a lot of you lately, but is there any chance you can stay late today? I have a lot to discuss with my husband and father."

"Of course! I can stay as long as you need me."

"In that case, instead of spoiling their appetite with a snack, why don't you go ahead and feed the girls dinner? Maddie left a chicken-and-rice casserole warming in the oven. There's plenty for you as well."

Becca's face brightened at the mention of free food. "That sounds perfect. Thanks."

Ellie was distraught at the sight of her reflection in her bathroom mirror. In addition to her tangled hair and the angry marks on her neck, her face was pale and drawn, with purple half-moons as dark as bruises under her eyes. This predicament with her sister was taking its toll. She longed to crawl in her bed, pull the covers over her head, and sleep until the crisis was resolved. Instead, she splashed water on her face, dabbed on some makeup, and changed into fresh clothes. Hoping the vibrant colors would lighten her mood, she chose a pink cotton T-shirt and Lilly Pulitzer capris.

Downstairs, she discovered that peace had been restored. Lia was gone. Robbie was once again perched on the settee, looking alert. And her father was deep in conversation with Julian in his study. Both men stood when she entered the room.

"You're so pale," Julian said, rushing to her side.

"Gee, thanks. I put on makeup and everything."

"Here, come sit down." Julian gripped her arm as though she might fall and escorted her to the sofa. "This will help." He poured two fingers of amber liquid into a crystal glass and handed it to her.

"I'm fine, honestly. Just a little shaken up. Nothing a good shot of bourbon won't cure." She downed the bourbon in one gulp.

"Atta girl," Julian said, and poured more liquid in her glass.

She relaxed against the soft leather cushions. "Where'd she go?"

"I took her to the Days Inn on Meeting Street," Abbott said. "I paid for one night and gave her the contents of my wallet, suggesting strongly that she use the money to buy a ticket on the first mode of transportation out of town tomorrow morning."

Ellie grunted. "That's not likely to happen."

Abbott hung his head and stared into his drink. "No, I'm afraid you're probably right."

"She's a monster." Julian crossed the room and closed the door for privacy. "After what happened here today, I'm genuinely concerned for the safety of all our children. Poor Ruby. How is she?"

"She's calmer now. We had a good talk. She's quite a remarkable child." Ellie smiled at the thought of her foster child.

Julian sat down close to Ellie. "I'm at a loss as to where we go from here. I thought that hiring a security guard was a good solution. A lot of good he was."

"In Robbie's defense, he took his lead from me," Ellie said. "I told him I could handle it. He had no way of knowing she'd go berserk. None of us did."

"Well, it won't happen again," Julian said. "I had a little talk with Robbie. He is to contact the police immediately if he sees Lia anywhere near our property. Under no circumstances is he to let her inside this house."

"Maybe you should pack up the kids and go stay in a hotel," Abbott suggested. "At least until after the hearing on Thursday."

"That would scare the children. I refuse to be run out of my own home." Ellie left the sofa and went to stand in front of the fireplace. She lifted her grandfather's mahogany jogging stick off the mantel and gripped it tight in her hand. She could still feel the sting of the jogging stick against her tiny bare legs. She'd seen the wicked glint in her sister's eyes when she'd attacked her in the hallway. Lia was cut from the very same cloth as her grandmother. She carried the insanity gene, if there even was such a thing. She restored the stick to the mantel and turned to face her husband and father. "I think we should help her."

Their jaws dropped simultaneously.

"Are you out of your mind?" Julian asked.

Abbott said, "Help her do what, honey?"

"Get her the psychiatric help she needs to control her bipolar disorder or whatever disorder she has."

"I don't understand. Why the sudden about-face?" Julian asked.

"Because a very wise little girl upstairs just reminded me that family is family. We don't choose our siblings. We're born from the same parents. Lia and I are not just sisters. We're twins. If I were the one with emotional problems, I would want someone to save me from myself. She has no one else. I'll never be able to live with myself if I don't at least try."

Julian reached for the decanter beside him and poured more brown liquor into his glass. "The question remains . . . how do you intend to help her? You can't drag an unwilling person to the psych ward."

"I realize that, Julian." She walked back to where they were sitting and stood looking down at them. "I'd like to speak with her in mutual territory, somewhere where we can talk calmly and rationally while I present my offer. If she's willing to be hospitalized, I will continue to take care of the twins for however long it takes for her to get better. When the doctor deems her stable, I will give her the money to buy a house here in Charleston and help her pay the bills until she can find a job she enjoys."

Julian and Abbott stared at her, speechless.

Ellie continued, "It's a win-win situation for everybody when you think about it. Lia gets healthy and she gets to keep her children. Meanwhile, we get to be a part of the twins' lives while keeping a close eye on their mother."

"I don't know, sweetheart," Abbott said, shaking his head. "After what I've witnessed these past few days, I'm not sure Lia will ever be right no matter what mind-altering drugs the doctors give her." She started to object, and he held his finger up, silencing her. "But I see how much this means to you, so I'm willing to go along with it on the condition that neither you nor the twins are alone with Lia until she's . . . until she's cured, for lack of a better word."

Julian sat back on the couch and crossed his arms over his chest. "I'm skeptical, and I'll continue to be skeptical until I see dramatic improvement in her behavior. I realize the decision is not ultimately mine, but until that time, I would prefer the twins not see her at all."

Ellie nodded. "I think that's a smart move."

"And under no circumstances is she allowed in this house," Julian added.

"I insist on being present when you talk to her," Abbott said. "How do you plan to approach her with your proposition?"

"We go to her motel first thing in the morning and request a meeting."

LIA

*L*ia's eyes opened wide at midnight, on the dot, according to the digital clock on the table beside her bed. She'd slept a solid seven hours, the most uninterrupted sleep she'd had in months. Forging her way through the fog that threatened to swallow her whole, she forced herself to sit upright. She teetered on the precipice of the abyss. She couldn't give into despair now, not when she was on the verge of getting everything she'd ever wanted. Freedom. All the material goods that money could buy. The seductive lifestyle that came with being wealthy. Tomorrow, she would figure out how to get her hands on her money. Tonight, she would settle for sex.

She showered for the first time in days and slipped into a low-cut, black knit dress that clung to her curves and left little to the imagination. She fashioned a gauzy red scarf around her neck and crammed her feet into black stiletto heels. Aside from a bite of a stale sandwich, she hadn't eaten in over forty-eight hours. But she had no appetite for food. She aimed to satisfy the desire in her loins, not the hunger in her gut.

She stuffed the money Abbott had given her in a cross-body bag and set out on foot toward the waterfront. The going was slow and unsteady, tramping in stilettos on brick sidewalks and cobblestone streets, but she eventually arrived at a dive bar with classic rock-and-roll music blaring from inside and a crowd of patrons spilling out into the street. She nudged her way through the mob to the bar and ordered a glass of wine, her first alcoholic beverage since she'd left Justin. She needed a numbing agent to chase the blues away. She knew it was inevitable, when she stopped taking her medication, that the day would come when her moods would shift and force her to face her demons.

How long will it last this time? Weeks? A month?

She'd survived the depths of depression before. She'd survive this time as well. One thing she knew for certain—she'd become an alcoholic or a nymphomaniac before she went back on lithium.

She lifted her shoulders back and held her head high.

Think positive, Lia. The demons have to catch you before they can drag you down.

She drained her glass of wine and grabbed the man standing next to her by the arm, pulling him onto the dance floor. Her body moved to the beat of the music as she twirled from one man's arms to another's. She finally settled into a pair of sinewy tatted-up biceps. He pressed his rock-solid body against hers. He was just the antidepressant she needed.

ELLIE

Once again, Abbott stayed the night in Ellie's guest room. With Lia on the loose, Ellie felt better knowing all her loved ones were under one roof—with Robbie standing sentry over them. Ellie, Julian, and Abbott stayed up talking until almost midnight in the study, and then Julian and Ellie continued the discussion once they'd retired to their bedroom. It took some convincing, but Julian eventually agreed to support her plan. At least for the time being.

Shortly after dawn, Abbott went home to shower and shave. He was drinking coffee with Maddie in the kitchen when Ellie came downstairs a few minutes before eight. She wore her auburn hair pulled back in a tight bun and a loose-fitting cotton sheath in a somber shade of slate gray that she deemed appropriate for the occasion.

Maddie handed her a mug of coffee. "I don't like it one bit, Miss Ellie. You playing with fire. Your sister is evil, just like your gramma. I been telling you that. But you's too stubborn to listen."

Ellie noticed four sets of wide eyes watching them from the table. "Shh, you're frightening the children," she said in a low voice. "There's a good chance my grandmother was bipolar. They didn't know much about the disorder back in her day."

"Nah," Maddie said, shaking her head with vehemence. "Your gramma didn't have no disorder. She was just plain mean. Lia too. Ain't no doctor in no hospital gonna be able to fix her."

Ellie reached for her old friend's hand and squeezed it. "I appreciate your concern, Maddie. I truly do. But I have to do what I think best and pray everything works out the way it's meant to."

Maddie studied her in an unnerving way that made Ellie feel like a little girl again. "I understand." She looked away from Ellie to Abbott. "You take care of my girl now, ya hear? Anything happens to her, and I'm coming after you."

"Yes, ma'am." Abbott saluted her. "I promise we'll be careful."

Ellie took time to go over Katie's homework assignments, compliment the twins on their latest coloring masterpieces, and help Ruby gather her belongings for school.

"We'll drop you at school on our way," Ellie said to Ruby as she tucked her lunchbox in her backpack. Peninsula Elementary was out of their way, but she didn't want the child walking to school all my herself with Lia on the loose.

Abbott carried Ruby's backpack out to the car for her. As he helped her get settled in the back seat, he said, "With all these children, I think Miss Ellie needs a bigger car, don't you?"

Ruby giggled and nodded her head.

"You sound like my husband," Ellie said as she backed out of the driveway. "We've been shopping for mommy cars, but I'm having a difficult time parting with my Mini. It comes in handy when trying to find a parking place."

On the way to school, they talked about which SUVs and station wagons she was considering and the advantages of having a bigger car. When they arrived at Peninsula Elementary, Abbott got out of the car and walked the child inside.

Ellie rehearsed what she planned to say to her sister while she waited for her father to return. When he slid into the passenger seat, she threw the car in gear.

"Let's get this over with."

She navigated the car back to Meeting Street. As they neared the motel, a convoy of police cars and fire engines approached from the opposite direction. Traffic slowed to a crawl.

"Is that Lia's room?" Abbott said, craning his neck as he stared through the front windshield up to the second floor of the motel.

Ellie followed his gaze to the cluster of policemen gathered outside a room at the far end of the exterior corridor.

"Damn! That is Lia's room." Abbott jumped out of the car and dashed across the street.

Ellie parked haphazardly in a no-parking zone and joined her father at the bottom of the concrete stairs leading up to the second floor. The police had marked off the staircase with yellow crime-scene tape. Abbott begged information from every policeman that brushed past them until he found a plainclothes detective willing to listen. "Can you tell me what's going on? My daughter's in room 260."

"Are you certain of that, sir?" According to the badge he wore on a chain around his neck, the detective's name was Lambert.

"Yes, I'm certain," Abbott said. "Has something happened to her?"

"Come with me, please." The detective led them into the motel office, which was empty aside from the lone desk clerk—a man in his forties who wore his hair in a braided ponytail and an expression of distaste on his craggy face. "Can you tell me your daughter's name, sir?"

"Lia Bertram. I paid for her room myself, late yesterday afternoon. He was here," Abbott said as he gestured toward the desk clerk. "He can vouch for me."

The desk clerk nodded his confirmation.

"Has something happened to my sister, Detective?" Ellie

blurted.

"I'm afraid so, Mrs. . . ."

"Hagood. Ellie Hagood. Lia is my sister." Ellie found it difficult to breathe. "Please, Detective! Tell us what happened to her."

"I'm sorry to be the one to break the news. The maid discovered her body this morning. It's premature to say for certain, but it appears as though she was murdered."

Ellie gasped. "Murdered? Who would do such a thing?" As the words parted her lips, she realized there were at least three people with plenty of reason to want her dead.

"That's what we're going to find out." The detective ushered them into the corner of the office for privacy. "I'm Detective Lambert with the Charleston PD. I questioned Lia earlier in the week regarding . . . another matter."

"We're aware of the investigation into her husband's death," Abbott said. "I hired her criminal attorney, Gary Bates, myself."

A horrible thought crossed Ellie's mind and sent a chill up her spine. "I spoke with Detective Hamlin yesterday afternoon. He believes Ricky Bertram's death was a result of his gambling debts. Do you think there's a chance Lia's murder might be related to her husband's?"

"I don't believe so, although it's too early to say for sure. It appears your sister was strangled to death during the act of sexual intercourse."

Ellie gulped back the taste of bile. "How awful! I wasn't aware she was seeing anyone." There was so much she didn't know about her sister.

"I understand you're in shock, but we need a family member to make a positive identification of the body," Lambert said. "Do you think you could do that now, or would you rather do it sometime later today?"

Ellie didn't trust her voice to speak. She was glad when her father said, "No sense in holding up your investigation, since I'm already here."

"You can't actually go into the crime scene," Lambert said, "but you can see enough from the doorway to make a proper identification."

Abbott started for the door. When Ellie stepped in line behind him, he held his hand out. "You stay here, honey. I got this."

"Not a chance, Dad," she said, and walked on ahead of him. She'd never seen a dead person before. As much as she hated to have this lasting image of her sister, she needed to see for herself that the person in the motel room was in fact Lia.

Ellie and Abbott followed Detective Lambert, single file, up the concrete steps and down the corridor, stopping at the threshold of room 260. Ellie inhaled a deep breath, bracing herself, as she stared into the room at the dead body lying stark naked on the king-size bed. Lia's eyes were wide open, her expression frozen in fear. Her complexion was pasty, her lips tinged blue, and bruises marked her neck where the killer had squeezed the life out of her.

She turned away and fled the scene. She ran back down the corridor, taking the steps two at a time to the parking lot. She was doubled over, hands on knees, sucking in air to force back the urge to vomit when her father found her minutes later.

"I tried to warn you, sweetheart," he said, resting his hand on her back.

She straightened. "I needed to see her, Dad, for the sake of closure. But it doesn't make it any easier."

"I know, baby." He drew her in for a hug. "I envisioned this whole nasty ordeal playing out in a million different ways, but this was never one of them."

Detective Lambert caught up with them. "I'm very sorry for your loss. I have some questions I need to ask you. I'd appreciate it if you'd come down to the station whenever you're feeling better. Sometime today would be best, if you can manage it."

Ellie pulled away from Abbott. "I'd like to get it over with as soon as possible," she said to her father, and then to the detective, "When would be a good time?"

"I'm headed to the station now, if you're up to it."

"We'll meet you there," Abbott said.

As THEY HURRIED across the street to the car, Ellie rummaged through her bag for her keys and her phone. She handed Abbott the keys and tapped out Julian's number. When she heard her husband's voice, she burst into tears, and the words spilled from her lips.

"Lia's been murdered." Unable to continue, she thrust the phone at her father, who explained the situation to her husband.

Julian and Robbie were waiting for them at the station when they arrived. Julian held his arms open, and she collapsed into them. "It's all over now," he said in a soft voice. "Everything is going to be all right."

"Since September, when I learned of Lia's existence, I've been on an emotional roller coaster of extreme highs and lows. I don't even know what to think or feel anymore. I feel relieved that the ordeal is over. And guilt for feeling relieved. Who would've done this to her, Julian?"

"Certainly not anyone who cared about her. My guess is she picked up the wrong guy in a bar somewhere. You have nothing to feel guilty about. Lia was a virtual stranger to you, and you gave her money and took in her children. She never once expressed an ounce of gratitude in return. She was a sick woman, baby. You were so hopeful about getting her psychiatric help, but the truth is, I'm not sure how receptive she would've been to that help. We were facing a lifetime of dealing with her drama. I'm not sure how long we could've sheltered the twins from her. If the judge had ruled in Lia's favor . . . well, I can't even bring myself to think about what kind of life they would've been forced to live."

She tilted her head back to look at him. "My sister was murdered, Julian. I agree that we're all better off with her dead. But admitting that makes me feel guilty. I can't help that."

"Don't look at it that way, baby. You didn't kill Lia. She made a fatal error in judgment. That has absolutely nothing to do with you. You spent most of last night scheming ways to help her while she was off whoring around somewhere. That sounds callous of me, I know. But she certainly wasn't worried about you last night. Or Bella or Mya. Feel sad. Or angry. Or any number of other emotions. But not guilt. Now that she's out of the picture, we'll be able to adopt the twins and raise them in a safe and loving home. Do I feel guilty about that? Hell no."

She planted her face in his chest. "It's easier for you. She wasn't your sister."

"Maybe so." He exhaled, and his breath tickled her neck. "I resented what she was doing to you, the way she'd turned our lives upside down. I never shared your pity for her. I never would've wished her dead, but I sure as heck was praying she'd go away and leave us alone."

Abbott approached from behind and tapped Ellie on the shoulder. "Detective Lambert is ready to talk to us now. If you're not up to it, we can come back later."

She pushed away from Julian. "I'll be fine." She searched in her bag for a tissue. "Give me a minute to run to the restroom."

Abbott smiled at her, his dark eyes warm with compassion. "Take your time. I'll wait for you here."

In the ladies' room down the hall, Ellie blew her nose, splashed cold water on her face, and smoothed stray hairs back into her bun. She inhaled and exhaled several times to collect herself.

Do this for the twins, Ellie. They're counting on you. You're their mama now.

Lambert was waiting for her when she returned to the reception area. He showed them to an interview room where Ellie—

with frequent input from her father—spent the next several hours reliving the events of the last seven-plus months. They drank cup after cup of bitter coffee and took multiple bathroom breaks, mostly for Ellie's benefit so she could regain her composure after a particularly emotional testimony. About halfway through, Robbie and Julian were summoned in to vouch for their where-abouts during the previous evening at the supposed time of the murder. Lambert was summoned from the room three times by coworkers with updates from the ongoing investigation. Upon his return each time, he reported what he'd learned. The surveillance footage from the motel was being reviewed. A bartender at a popular late-night establishment on the waterfront reported seeing a woman matching Lia's description sometime after midnight. The man she left the bar with had been identified and was being pursued.

Ellie was exhausted and hoarse by the time they finished, but the process was therapeutic in helping her fully grasp the sacri-fices she'd made for her sister.

Lambert was showing them to the door when he received word that the man was in custody and had confessed to the crime.

"He claims he didn't mean to kill her," Lambert told them when he got off the phone with his partner. "With Lia's consent, he was experimenting with asphyxiation in an effort to heighten her orgasm. He took it too far. Sadly, it's not the first time that's happened." The detective handed Ellie his business card. "We'll be in touch if we have additional questions. Feel free to contact me if I can be of help in any way. And, again, I'm terribly sorry for your loss."

His words felt empty after all she'd told him about Lia.

Do I even have the right to mourn my sister?

Perhaps she would mourn what could have been.

ELLIE

*E*llie, wanting to talk to Julian, gave Abbott the keys to her Mini so he could drive Robbie home. She dreaded the task of telling the children. "I have no idea how to handle this situation. What do I say to them?" she asked on their way home from the police station.

Julian took his eyes off the road and glanced over at her. "Why do you have to tell them anything? The twins are way too young to understand. One day, and you'll know when the time is right, you can explain everything to them—about their mother's mental illness and their father's death. There are plenty of lessons for them to learn from all that happened when they're old enough to handle the truth. As for Katie and Ruby, we simply tell them the judge granted us custody of the twins. Speaking of which . . . I spoke to Tyler while you were meeting with Lambert and explained the situation. If you're up to it, he'd like us to keep our appointment for court tomorrow. We're already on the docket. We might as well formalize the adoption."

That brought a smile to her face. "At last, a bit of good news." The smile disappeared as the enormity of the responsibility weighed on her. "Do you think I'll make a good mother?"

"What're you talking about? You already are a good mother—the best mother I know."

She stroked his leg. "Thanks for your vote of confidence. Our mixed brood makes for a happy and loving family, and I wouldn't have it any other way."

He smiled over at her. "And I couldn't love you more than I do at this moment."

MADDIE AND CILLA prepared an elaborate cookout for them that evening, with everyone's favorites: chicken and steak for the adults, and hamburgers and hotdogs for the children. Abbott invited Lacey, and Ellie insisted Maddie, Cilla, Robbie, and Becca join them. They'd gone to too much trouble for Ellie to object to the cookout. Instead of thinking of it as a party, she regarded the gathering as a wake, an opportunity for family to mourn. She spent a moment at the edge of the garden, near the rosebushes. Pressing her hands together, she closed her eyes, tilted her head toward heaven, and said a prayer for eternal life and peace ever after for her sister.

They sipped cucumber martinis on the terrace while the children chased one another around the yard. Ellie experienced a moment of panic when she realized the squeals had stopped and the children were nowhere to be seen.

They're safe, Ellie. No one's going to hurt them now.

She searched the back yard and discovered the four of them camped out beneath the meandering branches of the magnolia tree. She crawled in with them.

"I spent a lot of time here as a child," she told them. "I used to think of this tree as my friend."

"Didn't you have any other friends?" Katie asked.

"Only one," Ellie said, thinking about the twin sister who had been taken from her when she was only three. "I was lonely a lot of the time when I lived here as a child." She stroked the nearest branch. "I confided all my secrets to this wonderful old tree. She's a good listener, a good secret keeper too."

Katie and Ruby giggled and tossed handfuls of magnolia leaves at Ellie. The twins joined in for a good old-fashioned leaf fight. Spent from exertion and laughter, she lay flat on her back and stared up the trunk of the tree to the darkening sky beyond. The twins curled up to her on one side, and Katie and Ruby on the other. She gathered the four of them in her arms as best she could and closed her eyes. Her dream had finally come true. She never thought she'd have any children. God had blessed her with four.

THEY HAD much to celebrate during their week at Sullivan's Island in June. By then, they'd learned from Franny that Ruby's mother had been sentenced to fifteen years in prison, and the paperwork for Ellie and Julian to adopt the child had been filed with the court systems. No one was surprised when Katie's mother, Laura, was fired from her job in Spartanburg, but she shocked them all by accepting a position all the way across the country, in Seattle. Her decision to move out of state nullified her parental rights, thereby granting Julian full custody. Although Katie would undoubtedly miss her mother, Ellie suspected she was secretly relieved at the outcome. Katie and Ruby had both been accepted to Ashley Hall for the fall term, and the twins would be applying for kindergarten the following year.

They filled their days on Sullivan's with pleasurable activities while setting aside plenty of time to relax. They rode bicycles all over the island and drove a golf cart, which Julian had rented, to the small village for lunch. Becca, a certified swim instructor, worked with Ruby every afternoon in the kidney-shaped pool that belonged to the cottage and taught the older girls how to sail the sunfish she'd trailered to the island. They walked the beaches, searching for shells, and built elaborate castles in the sand. At night they roasted hotdogs and marshmallows in the small bonfire Julian built near the sand dunes. Abbott brought Lacey, whom Ellie was beginning to think of as a friend, down for a long weekend. When Ellie and Julian saw how much their family enjoyed their time on Sullivan's, they agreed to start working with a realtor to find a place of their own.

Ellie was delighted that Maddie agreed to accompany them as their guest on their family vacation. She made their beds in the morning and put out baked pastries for breakfast, but she spent the majority of the week fishing off the end of the dock.

For two weeks, she and Maddie had been dancing around the subject of Lia's death. Ellie sensed her old friend had something on her mind, and late one afternoon midweek, she decided it was time to find out what that something was. She ventured down to the dock with two glasses of sweet tea. She handed Maddie a glass and sat down on the warm cypress boards next to her with her feet dangling over the side.

"Where are all the fish you've caught?" Ellie asked, searching the dock for a cooler. "I've been watching you reel them in."

"I threw 'em all back. No sense in keeping them itty-bitty spots and croakers. I'm gonna catch me a great big flounder and fry him up for your supper."

Ellie laughed. "Fried flounder sounds yummy as long as you promise to make some of your homemade coleslaw and corn-bread to go with it."

Maddie cackled. "You're on."

They sat in silence for a while, enjoying the salty breeze, watching the boats speed up and down the sound, and listening to the joyful sounds of the girls playing Marco Polo with Julian in the pool.

"I have to give you credit, Maddie. You were right about Lia all along."

Ignoring Ellie's gaze, Maddie stared down into the muddy water of low tide. "I wanted to be wrong about her. I truly did. To this day, I never understood how twins can turn out so different. You and Lia were night and day. Even as a young'un, you shone from the light within. But Lia, that poor chile, she could never escape the dark cloud that followed her around."

Ellie allowed her mind to travel back decades. "I don't remember her that way."

"Because you could never see that side of her. She was your twin, your only playmate. You had no one to compare her to."

"I hadn't thought of it like that."

"I promised your mama on her deathbed that I would look out for you. But I knowed it was for the best when your daddy came to take you away. You had no bidness living in this house with your mean old gramma. Mr. Abbot's a kind man. He gave you a good life." Maddie patted Ellie's knee. "But I was beside myself with happiness when you found your way back to me. I'd do anything for you, Miss Ellie. I hope you know that. But when Miss Lia showed up . . . well, I couldn't live through that hell again. I had to protect them twins, those sweet little girls."

Ellie jerked her head up. "You sound like you had something to do with my sister's death."

"I don't have that kind of power, but I know someone who do. I visited an old Gullah woman. Some say she's a witch. I didn't ask for her to bring death to Miss Lia. But I did ask for her to keep Miss Lia away from them twins. If God wants to lock me out of heaven because of what I did, then so be it. But I ain't gonna apologize for my feelings. I seen too much sadness in that house."

Ellie reached for Maddie's hand and squeezed it. She didn't know much about Gullah culture, but she certainly wasn't one to question centuries-old practices. "You were not alone in this, Maddie. None of us wanted her to die, but we all wished Lia would go away and not come back. You're a kind and compassionate woman. You've stuck by this family through our darkest days. The Lord won't lock you out of heaven. He knows how much love you have in your heart."

"You got the same kind of love in your heart, Miss Ellie. Just like your mama. You will be a kind and caring mama to all four of them little girls, like your mama never got a chance to be to you."

ACKNOWLEDGMENTS

I'm grateful to the many people who helped make this novel possible. First and foremost, to my editor, Patricia Peters, for her patience and advice and for making my work stronger without changing my voice. To my literary agent, Andrea Hurst, for her guidance and expertise in the publishing industry and for believing in my work. A great big heartfelt thank-you to Kathy Sinclair, former social services special investigator and current criminal investigator with the Bartow County Sheriff's Office, for her expert advice and guidance in matters relating to adoption, foster parenting, and the murder investigation. And also to my sister-in-law Dina Farley Foster, attorney-at-law and former family court judge, for patiently explaining the judicial system and social services procedures in regards to child abandonment and the placement of children whose parents have been imprisoned for serious crimes.

To my faithful readers for their support of my work and for giving me the confidence to write from my heart. And to Damon Freeman and his crew at Damonza.com for their creativity in designing this stunning cover.

I am blessed to have many supportive people in my life who offer the encouragement I need to continue my writing career. I owe a huge debt of gratitude to my advance review team for their enthusiasm of and commitment to my work, to my family and friends for their continued support and encouragement. A special note of thanks to Leslie Rising at Levy's and the folks at Grove Avenue Pharmacy in Richmond for spreading the word about my books and to Alison Fauls for being the best beta reader ever.

I love hearing from you. Feel free to shoot me an email at ashley-hfarley@gmail.com or stop by my website at ashleyfarley.net for more information about my characters and upcoming releases. Don't forget to sign up for my newsletter. Your subscription will grant you exclusive content, sneak previews, and special giveaways.

ABOUT THE AUTHOR

Ashley writes books about women for women. Her characters are mothers, daughters, sisters, and wives facing real-life issues. Her goal is to keep you turning the pages until the wee hours of the morning. If her story stays with you long after you've read the last word, then she's done her job.

Ashley is a wife and mother of two young adult children. She grew up in the salty marshes of South Carolina, but now lives in Richmond, Virginia, a city she loves for its history and traditions.

Ashley loves to hear from her readers. Feel free to visit her website or shoot her an email. For more information about upcoming releases, don't forget to sign up for her newsletter at ashleyfarley.net/newsletter-signup/. Your subscription will grant you exclusive content, sneak previews, and special giveaways.

ashleyfarley.net
ashleyhfarley@gmail.com

80995925R00139

Made in the USA
Middletown, DE
18 July 2018